THE DEVIL'S
INTELLECT

*This book is dedicated to Jackie and Jason Isbell because
without them my story would have not been finished.*

AuthorHouse™
1663 Liberty Drive
Bloomington, IN 47403
www.authorhouse.com
Phone: 1-800-839-8640

First published by AuthorHouse   07/28/2011

ISBN: 978-1-4634-4530-0 (sc)
ISBN: 978-1-4634-4529-4 (ebk)

Printed in the United States of America

Any people depicted in stock imagery provided by Thinkstock are models, and such images are being used for illustrative purposes only. Certain stock imagery © Thinkstock.

This book is printed on acid-free paper.

THE DEVIL'S INTELLECT

JENNIFER ISBELL

authorHOUSE®

CONTENTS

As a child I was loved, I was nurtured but when Adam was born I instantly knew who would take my place. Adam and I were only two years apart and we only grew older only knowing love and kindness but, my mind set wasn't even in the realm of love for that bastard, he took my parents, my love and everything I ever had. I hated him so much and now it was my turn to take back what was rightfully mine, even if it meant killing him.

Chapter 1

the beginning

It was Christmas when the accident happened; Adam and I were on the pond an area that was forbidden by mother and father, but I didn't care I remember he was only six and I was eight, I slowly pulled him out into the middle of the pond, I then smiled and started dancing and singing an old nursery rhyme from school, "humpty dumpy sat on the wall, humpty dumpy had a great fall, all the kings horses and all the kings men couldn't put him back together again" Adam then started to do a little dance which resulted into him jumping and singing along, I at that time told him sternly to start jumping higher and harder, he simply shrugged his shoulders and did as I said, and at that the ice broke with a shattering sound and he was gone. I slowly knelled down and watched him thrash about, tiny air bubbles rose and fell, I watched as his tiny fists pounded the thick ice, not even making a sound.

There was no way in hell he could get out of that thick layer of ice, that is unless I helped him and honestly that was the last thing on my mind, 'to bring that little bastard back into my life, ha never'. I watched as bubbles fell from his lips slowly and his eyes widened and he seemed to stare straight through me, and in the instant I quickly stuck my arm through that bitter water and pulled his little ass out. If you ask me I don't know why I saved him, probably out of blindness, all I knew now was that I just screwed up my one and only chance to have my parents back and I just put him back into that tango of a life, how foolish of me.

His teeth chattered and his body was an indigo color, he slowly stood up and walked over to me and thanked me for saving him, or that is what I had imagined he just glared at me and started home in a frozen limp like walk. I obviously hadn't kept him under long enough.

When I walked through the door of the house I was accompanied by several slaps from mother, I stood there in shock as she kept hitting me. It was obvious that Adam told them and that's when they both started to fall apart 'mentally that is, and about me'. The doctor was at the door in minutes and the smell of him made me nauseous and sick to my stomach, so much pride in that man, you could sense it a mile away. Adam by then was fine, mother had made him soak in a warm bath then cuddled him by the fire, I on the other hand was beat from head to toe with a rolling pin, then was grounded for being near and on the pond, when I knew better and for endangering my brother's life. And Adam well, you can only guess he only received more and more attention, taking into account he was on the pond too. But it didn't stop there the rage and distaste in my mouth grew and grew igniting hate and an arrangement to finally rid of this nuisance in my way.

Later on in the evening mother had came to my room and sat dawn beside me, and only stared at me for what it seemed was a decade, she quickly fiddled with her fingers and looked at me in a way I can't even describe, it was a mixture of hate and love, joined together to create some sort of natural pity "Simon" she had said in a hushed voice, "Simon why would you knowingly put your brother's life in danger"? She asked this with such desperation nearly on the verge of tears. I just sat there fumbling my fingers and twitching my feet searching my brain for the correct words to spew out, I looked at her after several seconds, "I hate him, and he doesn't belong here, if he goes away we can all be happy again" I said this without a expression and deliberately shrugged my shoulders. At that a wail come from her gaping mouth and she rose her hand a slapped me several times, that is until my face burned like fire, she quickly called dad in and tattled on what I had said, I was then beat with the belt, this time harder and with every strike I could only think of Adam, and how he should be the one receiving this punishment not me.

That night I went to bed without supper and without any love at all from my parents, I was now completely invisible, though I couldn't sleep I just laid their thinking of Adam gone and what joy it would bring me and my parents. I must have fallen asleep because I woke to a banging noise inches away. I looked up to see mother packing all my stuff into my large brown suitcase, her eyes were puffy and her smile was a thin pressed line. "Mother where are we going"? I had asked in surprise. She only looked at me and started crying again, her makeup was already smeared and it was now running down her face. She then sighed and patted my head like some dog, and then left the room. Minutes later mother and father walked in both grim and tired looking, mother stood by him and I looked up to see her wiping her eyes with her sleeve, she smiled a fake smile and sighed, "son you are going somewhere special". Father was terrible looking and you could tell he had been up all night drinking again, his eyes pouted and under then large gray bags were formed, his usual smile was a thin pressed line, and to be honest it scared the hell out of me. Mother was wearing her light pink bathrobe with what I could imagine nothing underneath, her hair was a large puffy ball of red, and her eyes were red and swollen, from crying I'd imagined.

"Son" father had said with a deep sigh, he slowly sat down mother following, and before I knew it all three of us were sitting on my bed, mother and father hand in hand, me sitting there being stared at, they quickly exchanged glances and no joy overcame their sullen faces. Father than looked at me real hard, "Simon you do know we love you right"? I nodded. "And you know your mother and I only want what's best for you right"? I nodded once more, tears forming at the corners of my eyes. "Simon" mother finally said in a low voice, "you are going somewhere special, a place to help you". She paused and kissed my forehead, "you do want that, don't you son"? By now my mind and the world around me was frozen I could feel a cold shiver creeping up my spin into my eyes and nose, envy ran through my blood and hate boiled under my skin.

"But mom, please I . . . . I promise to be good, please don't send me away, I'll be just like Adam . . . please . . . please"! I know I played this real well because mother was on dad's lap crying like a helpless infant.

At that father slowly leaned down as if to kiss me, but stopped and sighed leaving the raw stench of booze, he stood up picked up mother and left me to myself.

Now I felt torn inside, my own parents were getting rid of me, for Adam's sake, because he was so much better than me, and I hated it, I hated him and most of all my parents. That night I was able to eat with the family, and then was sent to bed early while Adam stayed up and played games with mom and dad.

That night I couldn't sleep, or even close my eyes, I could only think of ways to rid of Adam, I lied in my bed for what it seemed was hours fascinating about Adams absence. The morning started abruptly, mother was running around the house like a chicken with it's head cut off, Adam was at the dinner table playing with his food like a baby, and I so badly wanted to go slap the crap out of him. Father was sitting by the fire sipping whiskey and reading the morning paper.

I sat down at the table and started to pour my cereal, then Adam started to scream and started to throw food at me than he deliberately slapped himself in the face, then begun to scream and shake his head while kicking his feet like a baby. I looked at him, "what is your problem"? I demanded, he just looked at me and screamed louder and louder until mother came running in her face white and her breathing unsteady. "What are you screaming about"? She yelled. He then stopped and wiped his eyes; "Simon slapped me, and threw food at me"! He said this without a hesitation, his eyes wide and his face all red. I looked at him not believing my ears, this little shit just made this all up to punish me again. Mother turned towards me, "Simon, what happened"? She asked her eyes glowering at me. "Mother I didn't do that"! I said honestly. She looked at me again, "do what"? She asked again. I looked at her, "slap him I didn't slap him, or throw food mom, I swear"! She then looked at Adam skeptically; Adam then started balling, worse than before, "mommy I'm telling the truth, he is, lying"! And at that she reached out and slapped me until father came running in, "what the hell is going on"? He asked his eyes red from the whisky, his feet stumbling. Mother stood up straight and looked at him, "Paul, he just won't stop hurting Adam". She cried. "Well what did he do"? Mother's eyes glistened, "he slapped Adam and was throwing food".

Father looked at me real hard, "is that what happened"? He asked. I looked up and without blinking and said, "NO!!! HE IS LYING, HE IS ALLWAYS TRYING TO GET ME INTO TROUBLE, YOU GUYS NEVER BEALIVE ME, AND NEVER LISTEN TO ME EITHER"!

Father shrugged his shoulders and looked at mother, "honey we don't know the truth, so how can we punish Simon"? He asked blankly. Mothers eyes widened, "oh hell no, my baby Adam would never hurt Simon, and how do you explain, the red mark on his face? He is lying, and I want him out of my house". She screamed deliberately staring at me. Fathers eyes shifted from mother to me, he sighed. "Simon, go to your room". He ordered.

I quickly bolted up the stairs but quietly kneeled down by the railing, listening on what their plans were. Father's voice was louder than before and he was shouting, "WHERE IS HE GOING TO GO, HUH? WE DON'T HAVE ANYONE WHO WILL TAKE HIM, WHY CANT YOU JUST FORGIVE, HIM? IF YOU WANT HIM GONE SO DAMN BADLY THEN YOU FIND A PLACE", and at that he left the room, breathing deeply and mumbling something. Mother eyes found me, like she knew I was their all along, a sly smile filled her face and then she picked up the phone dialed some number and looked at me the entire time she was talking, "oh that would be great, how about tonight"?

She then hung up the phone and called father back in, "aunt Bertines, is coming". She said then went into the living room and started reading. Father's eyes caught mine and he looked very sad, as if for some moment he didn't want me gone, then he lifted his hand and took another swig from his cheap whiskey and left the room. I slowly crept down the stairs, and mother's hand caught my wrist, "go get your shit ready she will be here in twenty". She demanded. I quickly bolted up the stairs and started packing all my stuff; I only had a few pieces of clothing so it didn't take me long, I packed my bone collection and all my rocks, my books and my blankets, though I knew aunt would have blankets already but I didn't care, it was mine and where ever I went my stuff would follow.

Aunt Bertines was an awfully round woman, she had a mop of bright red hair and the worst attitude, aunt wasn't a very nice person, and to be frank she was a bitch the very definition, always yelling, criticizing and she was mean, I remember on Easter, she pushed me so hard I broke my arm, and when I told my parents they beat me for lying and saying such a terrible thing, I was scared to go with her, and 'I knew my life was in jeopardy, the moment I would step into her house I would be sentencing my own death'.

She was at our door in less than five, and how she got their so fast, surprises the hell out of me, because she lives on the other side of London, and the only way here would be by train of car, and both weren't that fast unless she drove like a bat out of hell. She slowly opened the door, and instantly looked at me, "so this is him ... Simon, the one who hurts people". She said this all to fast, for me to actually understand. Mother nodded, "yes this is him". She said angrily. Mother and father packed my stuff in the trunk, and at that sent me away, with the wickedest women alive.

The entire way their neither of us talked, she basically slept the whole way their, her face all squashed up against the window, drool flowing from her gaping mouth. I just sat there staring off into the distance, blankly my head buzzing my hands sweaty my legs wobbling.

Aunt B. woke up when we hit the middle of London, she bought me several outfits, shoes and books, it scared me, why would this horrid hag, be buying me all this crap? Was it to lure me into trusting her? Or was it to be generally nice? Either way I didn't fall for it, I knew what she was capable of and I knew it well. When we entered the front gate, and I saw how big her house was I nearly shit my pants this place was like a castle compared to our little shack. When we entered the house, it was quite dark, and extremely quite, I was shown to my room, and told that I would have supper brought to me by one of her servants, and when she said servant I was relived, it was nice to know that I wasn't; entirely alone with this mad woman. She said that she was going to bed, and that I had better stay put in my room or else.

Chapter 2

Sinister duties

I didn't sleep the first night in the house I was way to scared to even close my eyes, the thought of being in the same house with her was killing me. I'm quite unsure how I was to feel about my new arrangement, was this, the end of the line for me? Or was I actually in a home where I would be loved? These were questions that only time itself would be able to answer. I must have fallen asleep because I awoke to the smell of hot food, and when I opened my eyes, in front of me on a silver platter was a bowl of eggs and some toast with jelly and orange juice, I was surprised because this was the first time I had ever eaten something so good, in our house all we had to eat was hot cereal that tasted like shit mixed with wheat. My mind froze when I saw all this; mother and father would have to work their entire lives to even be able to put food like that on our table. Now it was just lying there on a table in front of me without any strings attached. Even though I had a new life and was trying to be a new person, I still didn't forget about that little shit, Adam he had it coming, all the shit he caused, he was in for a big treat. But first I would let this new life play out, and when things became rough I would strike, and fast. Aunt B. called me down that morning, she stood at the foot of the stairs all dressed up, her hair was curled and they looked like small spirals, she smiled. "Morning Simon, I'm going into town, would you like to come with me? If you don't stay here and be good"! She said this in a rush of slurred words. She sighed, "Well Simon what will it be"? She asked, I could tell she was becoming impatient, "I'll play"! I said this rather quickly almost too fast for her to comprehend it. She then nodded and patted my head then left. I played outside most of the day, collecting neat rocks, and playing in the dirt, then I started to explore the house I found several neat and convincing hiding spots, and I found old pictures and boxes of rather old toys. Aunt B, arrived at around seven, she walked through the front doors with two people behind her both carrying colored boxes with satin ribbons on top. She glanced at me and smiled. "I bought you a few things Simon"! She smiled in an unkind way. She than straightened her back, and eyed me, "well Simon, don't you want to know what it is I bought you"? She asked this in an evil way, a smirk forming at the corners of her deep red lips. I nodded and walked over to her, her eyes grew dangerously wide and rage rushed through her, then she quickly pushed me knocking me onto the ground, with that she smiled nodded and went into her room.

I sat on the floor for several minutes, contemplating weather or not to cry or blow up, I just stood up and walked it off, and I quickly trotted up the stairs into my room.

It seemed like I was in my room for hours, and surprisingly no one came knocking that it until now,

"Simon, I've your lunch, please unlock your door"! I knew their was something weird and unusual about the voice, but I obviously didn't think enough, I opened the door not finding the sweet maid, but Aunt B, she was standing in my door way with that same wide eyed look. Her lips were thin and her cheeks were the color of fire, she quickly pushed me into my room shutting the door as she entered, 'I was scared, and I mean that'! She stopped as I hit the end of my bed, then she slowly pulled out a kitchen knife, then started waving it around my face, she started to stumble, then 'she was drunk' I couldn't smell it but I knew it lingered on her breath. I quickly stepped back, but she just kept coming forward, waving the knife ready to strike, she then stood up straight and before I knew it pain exploded through out my body, the knife was sticking out of my stomach, causing blood to spill out, I then hit the ground with a 'thud' and before I knew it all was black. I awoke to Aunt B, standing over me with a face full of sympathy, blood was smeared everywhere, and my body was throbbing so badly now, the knife then was in her hand again and she just stood their smiling. "That'll teach you boy, that'll teach you"!! She said this under her breath then left me to suffer. My stomach was now bright red and blood was flowing in a large stream, I tried to stop it but I was to weak, I just lied their in and out of conchesness, I opened my eyes to June, then she had me in her arms, white gauze was red and the blood still hadn't stopped, she patched me up as well as she could then fed me some pills, something to stop the pain. She looked at me then in pure raw sympathy, "boy you must steer clear of her, pretend she is a disease, stay away from her"!! She then smiled, and picked up the bloody bandages and left me.

As days passed June and I saw less and less of Aunt, she was like a ghost, she would be here than would vanish like some cheap magic trick, she became weirder and weirder, she locked herself in her room, she never ate or slept even in the middle of the night you could hear her screams and thrashing, she would throw things and make so much noise I would have to cover my ears it was very difficult to sleep in that house, I was afraid to close my eyes, thinking that I would open them to Aunt B, standing over me some other dangerous weapon in her fat hands. Aunt left the house more often now, and came home around midnight always drunk, slurring her words, falling over, she would go to her room and make tons of noise, then she would start screaming, I would wake several times to June's voice asking if she was ok.

June became my greatest friend, when I lived with Aunt; she would play games with me, read me stories, she loved me and I loved her twice as much. I remember once when Aunt locked herself in her room for two weeks without food, water. June said she was really scared for her, and that she had known Aunt for several years, always helping her get by, being her watch dog of a assort, but recently even before I came, she had just started acting weird one day, and from their she only went down on the line always coming home late and after hours, drunk and always stumbling around, never eating. "She scares me; sometimes I'm afraid to open her room, scared to find her dead in some dismay". She stopped and looked at me," and since you came, it's like she is only out to hurt you, if not kill you, and it just doesn't make sense to me". I sighed, "Maybe she just needs some real, psychological help"! I mumbled, she sighed, "maybe". At that I turned away and went to my room, I slowly opened my door and went to bed early that night.

Chapter 3

family matters

I woke that morning, like any other the house was cold, and I couldn't decide whether to go downstairs and see June, or stay up here clear of Aunt. June was at my door minutes after I woke, "you need to come down, Simon, and I have a surprise for you". I sighed and opened the door. I slowly trotted down the stairs and sitting on the couch was that horrid family I once had, all three sitting their legs crossed, hands intertwined. I looked at June, but to my surprise she didn't look at me, "Simon, they wanted to see you, they are your family". She sighed, then, left the room.

Mother came forth first, eyes red from crying, and it seemed that every time that I saw her she was crying or just finished. I looked at all of them and rage once again, circled through my veins. Mother was inches away then she opened her arms like I was going to hug her but automatically backed away, "oh Simon, I've missed you so very much, have you learned your lesson"? She asked this and in that moment I stared at her in disbelief, this bitch came all the way here not to get me but to ask if I had learned some damn lesson. Father was at her side in minutes the same emotionless expression played out on his face, "Simon, I believe your mother asked you a question, and I think you should answer", with that he slowly started to raise his hand to me, like before but different in a way. I quickly looked at Adam, who was sitting on the chair face all white, his eyes wide and shinny his lips curled in a shit-eating grin, what a bastard. At that I looked at them, and backed away. "Hell no, I don't ever want to go home with any of you ever again; I want you out of my life"!!! At that I ran up the stairs into my room, where I slammed the door and suffocated my screams into my pillow. I listened as the front door slammed and the car drove away, and in that instant no joy overcame me, no emotion just emptiness, a vast ocean of it and I hated it. June was at my door as they left, her face white, "Simon, I don't understand, they love you". She said this with pure stupidity, what did she know; she was just some stupid housemaid without even the slightest bit of knowledge. "You don't have to, besides it's none of your fucking business". I screamed at her then quickly ran to the door slamming it in her face. To be honest I wasn't sad or angry just shocked, that they would come all the way here to ask some dumb question, if I had learned my lesson, sure I have I learned that I fucking hated them all of them and if I had the chance right now I would rip their spines out and spit on their graves, but that would all come into play in time, time was the only thing holding me back from my sinister ways and duties. I felt extremely bad for June, I had taken my anger out on her, and I knew she was already dealing with a ton of stress from aunt. I found her downstairs in the kitchen she was leaned over the stove cooking what I think would have to be dinner, I tugged on her apron, she turned towards me, a question like face sticking out at me, "June I'm sorry about the way I acted, it's just that I don't like them, and I was just surprised to see them". I said this all in a rush of slurred words, my mind was crying for forgiveness, but my eyes were on fire like the rest of my body.

She stood up and pulled me into her arms, "oh Simon, its ok I forgive you, but we do need to talk". I looked at her, "about what"? I asked surprised. She sighed and walked over to the table, and sat down pulling me into the seat beside her, "Simon I'm leaving, my sister is very I'll and she has four kids, and well she needs me, and I've done everything possible here". I looked at her in rage, "so you're just going to leave? What about me what about aunt"? I screamed at her, my voice shaky from the tension. She looked at me than as if she was a baby, and like that tears poured, "Simon, it's not like that, I love you and I care for your aunt but I have family and they need me, and quite frankly they are much more important than . . ." She said all this in a hushed mumble. I looked at her, "more important than what, then what? Me more important than me, is that what you mean? You bitch"!!! At that she reached out and slapped me, then ran to her room, crying on the way. June left that night without even saying goodbye; she packed her stuff and never came back, now I was entirely alone with Aunt B in this old house, and to be honest I was scared, more than I had ever been, and I knew that the walls around me would instantly start to fall apart, and probably quicker than ever. That night I just lied in bed, my head was buzzing with curiosity for the morning, believe it or not, June's leaving played a large toll on me, I felt numb from head to toe, like I was some shadow without anything to cast it. I suppose I just didn't care anymore, how could I? I was an eight-year-old kid without a real loving family, I was alone, and damned in this hell of a world and Aunt was Satan. When I finally decided to close my eyes, I didn't dream I just went into a soundless slumber. When I woke that morning I was filled to the rim with fear, I slowly crept down the stairs, aunt was actually sitting at the dining room table, reading the paper and sipping what I had imagined would be some sort of alcoholic beverage. Her eyes flickered towards me and she was on her feet coming at me before I knew it her eyes were red, swollen with drunkenness and rage. I quickly took off up stairs, my feet stumbling trying not to fall and let her get an advantage on me, "don't you run from me, you little bastard, I'll kill you". She screamed at me, huffing while climbing the stairs. I made it to my room, and shut the door in her face then quickly locked it, that is until she started kicking the door, and with every hit I feared for my life. Several minutes later I listened as she walked down the stairs and out the front door, I slowly cracked the door open and peered out, scanning every area around, making absolute sure I wasn't going into any sort of ambush. I slowly crept down the stairs into the kitchen; I then grabbed a knife and walked into the living room, I looked everywhere and I just could not find her, 'she was nowhere to be found.' I was nervous, my bones ached and I felt sick, a sickness only caused by the greatest fear, the fear of not knowing where the hell Aunt was. I opened the door and found her standing in the driveway shotgun in hand staring up at the sky. Fear ran through my blood then like before but more, I then quickly shut the door locking her out. I didn't know what to do, I had this small knife and well she had a gun, either way both of our lives, mainly mine was in danger. I looked out the window and watched as the car roared to life; she backed up and left, I watched as the gate closed behind her with such easement. Relief surged through me and it felt so nice, I was now able to search the house and gather everything that would threaten my life. I slowly entered her room, everything was neat and tidy, but covered in at least an inch of dust, and it looked as if her room had been vacant for years. I went into her bathroom, the bathtub was filled with water, but the water was red and nasty, the rug was covered in matted hair which lied in large clumps, I backed away quickly, it was so nasty and smelt of death and blood, a lot of blood. I immediately went to the medicine cabinet, inside were several pill bottles, at that I popped off all the lids and counted the pills, and to my surprise not one pill was missing, she hadn't been taking her meds, and it was up to me to make her start.

Thing is I didn't know which pill did what, but I would have to take my chances, I then emptied at least a handful of every pill and stuck them into my pocket, I had a plan, I would empty her alcohol and mix the pills in everyone with some medical alcohol, I watched as every pill dissolved, and I knew that she would be entirely too drunk to even notice the difference, and by the time she drank the bottle down she would be on the floor in some seizure, and when the cops would come they would shake their sorry heads and say, 'well too bad, this woman asked for it if only she would have stopped drinking' they would shake their heads in pity and take the corpse away, and by then I would be on the road away from their on my way to finish off that retched family I still had.

That night I decided to stay awake, I sat on the chair in the living room, my eyes open and my mind on fire, I waited for hours and then she finally came home at around midnight, she stumbled in like before, her lips were frowning, and her eyes were once again blood shot, she then went into her room, but came out several seconds later and with her was a bottle of alcohol, not one of the ones I altered but one she hid in her room, I watched as she chugged the entire bottle, she then placed the bottle down and went back into her room, and in my complete surprise she never came out. I stayed down stairs that night, I sat in the chair in the living room, one eye open and one closed, staring at her room. I was so anxious for her to wake and chug a bottle of my alcoholic beverage. I then began to think of my future plans, after she died I would, or even while she was dying call the cops and report it then I would recover my hidden stash of money, which would total out to be at least twenty seven dollars, I would pack a few clothes and some bread, and be out on my way. I would then buy a train ticket to the other side of London, there I would find an apartment and settle down, get a job then live happily ever after. As I pictured this in my head I slowly started to drift off into sleep, I then quickly opened them and in front of me stood Aunt. B shot gun in hand finger on the trigger, the nozzle pointed towards me, I froze, I felt so numb like a statue, I didn't move I didn't blink, she then slowly closed her eyes and walked back into her room.

My heart was on fire, I couldn't breathe and my stomach was throbbing, I just sat there and didn't move, I watched that door all night, I couldn't, and wouldn't sleep that night and possibly never again not after that. Aunt hadn't come out of her room all day and for some reason I thought it was weird so as quietly and carefully as possible I opened her door, and on the floor lye Aunt, all sprawled out, her eyes were like marbles, glistening and gleaming, wide and near water like. Her red lips were now a dark purple and her mouth open wide like a large black hole waiting to swallow me whole, and beside her empty as can be was a bottle of my mixture, bone dry. I'm not stupid you know I know how to clean up evidence, I first wrapped my hands in plastic I yanked the bottle away from her grip and switched it out with the real liquor I emptied it and put it back in eth same position, the next part was quite tricky I had to get her lips on the bottle to make it look like she actually drank it so with much frustration I managed to get a perfect lip mark on eth rim at that I cleaned out the other bottle and dumped a little of the remainder in and swished it around I then threw it away with the plastic that was on my hands.

Chapter 4

death of the monster

As planned I packed my stuff and was on my way even before the cops showed up, I had never been in the city alone before so I found myself lost several times. When I found the train station, I quickly paid the ticket fee and boarded the train, the ticket wasn't even near the price I had imagined it to be, when I reached Top'el Tea's London, I bought a small apartment in an old apartment building, and it wasn't even expensive, it was large though, one bedroom a small kitchen a bathroom and a tiny living room. That night I slept the best I had ever had. The next day I paid my landowner, Anita twenty dollars to completely furnish and house my apartment. When I came home that day I walked into an exquisite house, everything was where it should have been, and frankly it was a nicer house than the one I lived in with my parents. Anita was a middle-aged woman, she had short brown hair and wore thick-rimmed glasses, and she hardly wore any makeup and usually dressed in long skirts and bright colored tops. I must have lived in that apartment for at least four months, I lived like a king that is until one day some officers came by my house and claimed I was the suspect for the sudden death of Aunt Bertines. I just stood there in complete shock, how in the entire world was this even possible? My legs suddenly collapsed and I fell to the ground, all was black at first, accompanied by a bright white light, colors swirling around than like it started it all went black. The nurse said I was out for three months and that I went into a temporary coma she claimed that their was something going on in my brain, something unpleasant but when she said this I almost chocked to death, I was tired and my memory was fuzzy and it scared me not knowing what had happened in the three months I was out. After another week or so some cops came by and hauled me away to the work house, I stayed in their for ten years, beaten and tormented by a vicious old hag named Mrs. Vilot`ue, she was the original owner and caretaker of the work house, by the time I was finally let out she was on her death bed, I believe she had cancer. Mother showed up then tagging along Adam, who was avoiding my eyes the entire time he was there, I was quite curious of why father wasn't with them, I then found out that he had drank himself to death, at that a vast ocean of sorrow filled my body, he was the only real person I had ever loved, and now, well now he was in his grave dead as the day. Mother told me that she had bought another house and that they were both living quite well, once gain anger surged through my veins, an in an instant I remembered everything, the hate the pain, the tears and the complete loneliness, and that's when I knew that I had just been given another chance, a chance to fulfill my duties, 'to kill Adam'. When I was finally let out of that horrid place, I had a sense of complete satisfaction and well being, I was stronger and older now and the world was at my feet. At that I found my house and to my surprise it wasn't touched, the place was clean, the bed made and not a speck of dirt anywhere. When I arrived at my apartment, Anita was outside, her brown hair now at her mid back, she smiled at me and leaped into my arms, "oh Simon, how have you been? You look so handsome, and well, I've missed you dearly". She laughed and then kissed the top of my head. Just like the first time I came to her when I was a child. That night I found it unreasonably hard to sleep, so instead I just sat there and thought about Adam, and the death of father, and how he had taken Adams spot. I received a job at the local meat market, for a dollar an hour for five hours, which wasn't something I could complain about I still had at least sixteen dollars left over from when I got here, and it was keeping my home a float for me. I'm not sure if it was the complete lack of love and nourishment never given to me when I was young, but whatever it was I felt it, was in my bones and ripping at my heart, now I felt so alone, and in this booming city I felt even more out of place. I went to the Oakland Cemetery on a Tuesday, to see my father's grave, I just stood on the wet grass, staring at the gray cross which marked his final resting place, a place for his body to be eaten by worms and maggots, he wasn't better off in their than in the world, there wasn't a place for him anywhere and it filled my heart with fire. And as I stood there no remorse overcame me no sorrow, or tears, I didn't bring any flowers or cards or candles, I came bare handed, and empty hearted, I came only to tell him the he had left me here all alone, once again. That night when I went home, I just sat in the kitchen thinking, contemplating whether or not to just end, it here, my life was in ruins, I had no family or friends and no one cared. I was just wasting away, and I knew I was better than that, better then this. The next day I didn't go to work, I woke up and went to the Local Pub, I then ordered a vodka with grape juice, that's when I noticed her, across the bar in a corner booth sat a woman, she had straw blonde hair and the bluest of eyes, she sat alone drinking what I had imagined would be a coffee. I just stared at her from across the bar, she was beautiful, and I wanted her, and I wanted her badly. I just sat there gazing at her, and the day I would get her, I would never share, she would be mine and only mine, and in a sense I felt selfish, extremely selfish. She left the bar at around dark, I followed her then, to her house, I was like her shadow 'invisible' and everywhere she went I followed, I was behind her in her tracks, 'surrounding her without her knowledge' then in an instant Adam was in front of her and I quickly jumped into the bushes, and watched, he approached her rather slowly and wrapped his arms around her waist and picked her up and swung her around, she laughed and kissed him, her mouth in perfect motion with his. She then quickly waved goodbye and went inside her house. Adam then started my way, "who is that, I know someone is in the bushes, come out"! He cooed. I slowly walked out in front of him, his eyes filled with rage and his lips twitched, he was angry and I loved it. "Hi Adam" I sang in an almost too loud of a voice. He quickly shoved me back, I fell then, or I should have, but see I knew he was going to push me so as I started to lose my balance, I quickly jumped out of the way, causing him to go forward, I knew he was going to fast so he tripped and hit his head on a tree. He bled for several minutes and finally passed out 'He's in a coma' or that was what I was hoping for, while he was lying in the hospital bed. I looked at him then and I knew that inside of him, wasn't human at all, he was a monster, a devil, something evil was festering inside of him and now I had finally put an end to it. Mother came running in then, her face grief stricken, and she immediately looked at me, "You son of a bitch" she screamed as she ran towards me, her hands wrapped around my neck and she started squeezing, my breathing slowed and before I knew it I was on the ground, several doctors holding her hands behind her back, dragging her out of the hospital. As she was being hauled out of the room I recited this to her.

"Do not fear what you are about to suffer, behold the devil is about to throw you into prison, that you may be tested, and for ten days, you will have tribulation. Be faithful onto death, and I will give you the crown of life"

Chapter 5

turn of tides

I was nearly out of this world when the nurse came to me and lifted me up off the ground, I then slowly took a seat next to Adam's bed, I just sat their staring at him, and I was so overjoyed with the sight of him. That night when I opened my front door, I was half expecting an ambush, but to my surprise, no one was there, only the darkness accompanied by the stale smell of rotting wood, and the bitter cold. I stood in the doorway for several minutes, contemplating whether or not to just go to the hospital and finish him off. That night I managed to get at least two hours of full sleep. I woke that morning with a body full of rage, I don't know why, the last few months, I hadn't had a dream, but now it seemed that all the ones I hadn't had, were all coming in at once, compacting my mind with memories, wants and all kinds of horrid thoughts. I left from work at lunch, I wasn't feeling well, I felt so ill, and I still didn't know why, my head was spinning and my limbs were shaking, I was shaking and my head was burning, and when I tried to close my eyes I would instantly vomit. When I called my doctor, she instructed me to be in her office in ten minutes, she took several tests and when she walked back into the room, her face was all wrong, she looked nervous, "Simon you have a mild case of scarlet fever" I looked at her, "Am I going to die"? I asked nervous. She sighed, "no, but I am going to prescribe you some meds". I looked at her, "how could I have gotten it"? "When you were in the work house possibly, it's an unsanitary place and it was probably festering inside of you for a while and now it just hit you"! She said this in a very scientific way. "So, is it treatable"? I asked. "Yes just make sure you have warm liquids like soup or cold foods like popsicles or milkshakes". She instructed." And keep your room moist which will keep your throat from getting too dry and sorer and make sure you take the antibiotics for at least 24 hours." she finished talking and sent me home. When I got home, I quickly popped some in my mouth and washed it down with milk, then want to bed early that night. I woke to someone knocking on my door, I quickly jogged to the door and opened it and standing there was Anita, "Simon, your brother he has awakened"! She panted. She quickly hugged me, "Oh Simon I'm so happy for you". She cried. I quickly pushed her back, "he . . . he is alive"? I asked in horror. She quickly nodded, "how did you come to know this"? I asked frustrated "your mother, she came by this morning and told me to tell you". I looked at her, and pushed her out the door, "she is no mother of mine, now leave"! I screamed. I was so angry that little shit was still alive but once again, I was given back my goal, 'to end his life' I went to the hospital then and asked for his room, when I opened the door, in the bed lye Adam, he was hooked up to several meters and needles, I slowly walked over to him, his eyes flickered open and he just stared at me just like the day on the pond, I slowly traced his iv's like they were piano keys, my fingers dancing across them. His eyes flickered to me than to the door, and back, a smile played across my lips, and in his eyes grew fear, 'fear of me, and what I was capable of" at that I exploded with laughter, he was finally afraid of me, and I envied it, the sense of it crawled up my nerves and chilled my bones. I was out of that hospital in less than two minutes, I walked home that night, I was annoyed, and the thought of Adam being so alive racked my nerves. When I finally opened my door, I was surprised to see mother, who was sitting in the living room, her skeleton hands folded in her lap her toothpick legs crossed, and I just looked at her and shut the door. She was in my face by the time the door closed completely, "You are no son of mine, you have taken everything from me, and I don't ever want to see your miserable face again, don't ever come around Adam again, or I'll . . . ." she muttered. "Or you'll what, huh, what will you do"? I asked in a sarcastic voice. She quickly raised her hand to slap me, but I quickly caught it, and I squeezed it hard, she then cried out in pain, I looked at her hard, "And if you ever come around my house again, I'll kill you, and believe me, I will". I said this in a calm voice. Her eyes grew wide and she yanked her hand back and without hesitation she left.

I just stood there, smiling with joy I sat in the kitchen for hours putting together a plan to rid of her and Adam, she took everything from me also, my love and she sent me away and gave my everything to Adam, and now it was my turn to turn the tides. That night I just sat in the kitchen, which seemed like hours on end I didn't go to work that day I wasn't even in the mood to put up with my bosses shit, I was still sick and it seemed like the antibiotics weren't helping but I took them anyway. I was so bored with my life, I didn't know what to do, and I was cold and tired, and invisible to the world. 'Can one be happy, when all else fails'? That's a question I asked myself several times. I was desperate for salvation, but eager to end everything, no one cared for me or about me, no one even knew I was here, I had no companionship, and it killed me inside, I only wanted to be cared for, 'was it too much to ask for'? I just wanted a caring family, like the ones you see in stores or in restaurant windows, I wanted that all of it, just something and someone that I could call my own, but I knew that it was too late and that I would never be given the chance to conquer that. The thought of mother in my house without my permission bugged me, so I went to find Anita, and ask her why she just let that woman into my home. I found her in the back hanging laundry; I walked up to her, "Anita, did you let that woman into my home"? I asked in a serious voice. She looked at me, "yes, she claimed that she was your mother and that you had been expecting her". She said this without looking at me. She glanced at me, "well why do you ask"? She asked. "Because, I wasn't expecting her, and I would like it if you wouldn't just let random people inside my home, family or not" I said this in an angry way, I wanted her to get the point I was coming across. I then turned away and went back inside, she was at my door by the time I was even inside, so I quickly opened it, "Why did you let her into my house, you have no right." I said bitterly, almost in a scream. She looked at me, "Simon that woman said you knew that she was coming by, so I let her in ". She said blankly. I looked at her, "well that was all I wanted to say, so you can go now". I said boldly. "There is something else we need to talk about, you are my only tenet, and frankly this business isn't working out like I thought it would so I'm going to sell this place so I can buy a house." She said this quite slowly. I looked at her in shock, "what, why?" I asked in utter confusion. "We'll see Simon I'm selling the entire building". She muttered. I looked at her in frustration my voice gradually increasing. "You can't do this, I've paid my share, and you can't just kick me out, you have no right"! she looked at me, "oh Simon, I'm not doing it to you personally, it's just that I'm getting older and well, this is a dead end business, I'm sure you understand". She gasped. I looked at her, "well I don't, and you won't take my house" I screamed. Her eyes grew wide and she quickly stood up and walked over to the stove, I quickly followed. She looked at me. "Well I'll have you know Mr. this decision isn't up to you to make, besides I own this place, so I'm leaving and tomorrow I'll come by, and hopefully you'll have a clear perspective on this matter." she said, her head tilted up. I looked at her, "I don't think you understand what is actually going on". I said angrily. She looked at me, "well how about you, tell me what is going on"? She said in a high pitched voice. I smiled and at that slowly raised an iron skillet from the stove and hit her over the head, at that she fell to the ground, with a loud 'thud' blood completely covered my kitchen floor, thick and red like velvet. By the time I dropped the skillet, she lay on the ground dead as can be, my head begun to spin, a weird sensation crawled up my nerves, and boiled in my veins. It was a good feeling, one of a kind, and the only one I'd ever had. I had successfully cleaned up the entire mess in about ten minutes and as for the body I threw it into the back dumpster, and burned all the rags with which I used to clean up the blood. I then washed the skillet and went to bed. I woke the next morning with a great sense of accomplishment, I was invincible, I cannot describe the feeling I received when I killed Anita, and to be honest even words can't describe it, pity possibly, or joy or even a tinge of spite. No one would come looking for her, and I had enough to pay the state for the taxes for the building so I had no worries. I believe it was about mid-night, when I decided to go to the East Side of London. I wasn't looking for anything or anyone, I went to the Local Pub, like usual I arrived by taxi, and I had a couple of drinks. Their weren't that many people that night, a few oldie's and a tall brown haired beauty, she had golden hazel eyes and was wearing a silver tank-top, with some light blue dress pants, accomplished with a pair of black planks. She looked amazing, I watched her from across the bar, studying her movements, my eyes were glued to her angel like perfection. And as you might have guessed, Adam came strolling up to her, he gently wrapped his arms around her shoulders and started to kiss her, he played with her hair wrapping his pointer finger around a lock of it, he than crouched down and whispered something into her ear, her eyes widened and she smiled accompanied by a slight nod to the head. She slowly stood up and followed Adam into the bathroom I was right behind them, I slowly eased into the bathroom and listened, in the front stall I listened as moans escaped, and several pleasurable screams followed. As I heard this I immediately wanted to jump in there and kill them both, but instead I slowly left the bathroom, after the last moan rage circulated throughout my veins and Hate exploded throughout my head, I wanted him in his grave and tonight I would put him there, and if she followed, I would end her life also, because nothing was going to come in-between my task tonight, 'nothing;' so I left the bathroom and went and had a couple drinks, it wasn't long before they both came out and had a couple more drinks. As I sipped my drink I imagined me sneaking up behind them both and killing them and the thought of it made my insides scream. Adam walked out of the bar first the young girl right behind him, I followed them as they slipped into a narrow alley way, he quickly pushed up against the wall of the building, unfastened his pants and tearing open her shirt, and from their you can only guess, I watched with pure fascination, never before had I seen something so strange but luring as that. As more moans escaped her mouth I quickly jumped out and slashed his throat, as expected the girl began to scream and then ran in a frenzy, I caught up to her as she approached a house, she quickly jumped the fence and opened the door locking it as she went inside. I sat outside her house for what it seemed was forever, I went home after it got dark, I burned my clothes, washed the knife and took a shower, after that I waited for the police. I had messed up real bad this time, 'she saw me and I saw her and right now she was probably calling the cops or already did'.

'Did she see my face', no! She couldn't have had . . . . , Right? 'Yeah, she couldn't, it was dark', 'was it dark enough'? I don't know, 'was it'? I racked my brain to the answers to these questions, smacking both sides, hoping it would just fall out. I was nervous, extremely nervous, how could I have let this happen, how could I have been so stupid? When the sun rose that morning, I wished I was dead, I knew that if I stayed inside, I would be considered suspicious, and that was the last thing I wanted, so I went to the pub and in the alley lay Adam, his body lye in a puddle of velvet blood, flies covered him and he looked pale, almost like the snow, and I knew he would be soon found, though I was curious of why he wasn't found that night, that girl knew he died, and I wondered why she never called the police. I quickly ran into the bar and in a frantic voice I told the bar tender to call 911 and that there was a dead body in the alley. Seconds later a police officer showed up, they gradually covered the body after they took several pictures, and then instantly came my way, "sir did you find the body"? A fat officer asked in a sharp voice, I nodded "your name sir"? He asked once more. I looked at him and then to Adam and sighed, "Simon, Sir Simon lucre". I spewed in a mellow voice. "Simon do you know this man"? He asked. I looked at him, "yes sir, he is my brother Adam". I said in an almost cry. The officer's face went white, "I'm sorry for your loss". He said slowly. 'But they had no idea, how sorry I was, sorry for not doing it earlier; I was happy, gleeful that he was finally dead and I was finally free'. The officer looked at me and sighed, "Well Simon keep, your phone nearby, you'll be expecting a call'. With that they took the body away and left. I noticed that the bar tender was eying me quite frequently, I quickly walked over to him, "do you have a problem"? I asked frustrated. He looked at me, "son you were in here yesterday, I saw you watching that man and I saw you follow him into that bathroom". He said in a mono tone. I looked at him, "well I'll have you know that that was my brother and that I had to pee, so if you have a problem with me going to your bathrooms, then tell me now". I said in a loud yell. His eyes widened and a deep gasp escaped his mouth. "Son, I wasn't being nosey and I'm sorry if I made you uncomfortable, and I'm sorry about your brother". He said in a sincere voice patting me on the shoulder. I looked at him in a sad way; I knew I was playing my cards well because his face was now a sullen sad fixture. "It's ok, I said in a sad voice, then left the bar. 'Adam's funeral was a few days' later, not many people attended; they all stood around the casket as it was lowered into the dark earth. I didn't dare show my face, mother would probably have a heart attack something I wanted to happen but not at a funeral, but that would be funny. I hid behind a tree feet away, I waited for everyone to leave the cemetery, I stood at the end of his hole, and just stood there, staring at the casket knowing he was dead, and that I was free. I then took a small pocket knife out and jumped down onto his casket than carved Simon into the top. I went home that night with a heart full of joy, pride and everlasting happiness, he was dead and there, was nothing anyone could do about it not now it was too late. I only had one more task and it was to rid of mother, but to do so would be fairly hard, 'I would let her come to me'. I would have to wait, and the moment she came to me, I would strike her dead. I slept quite well that night, soundless and soothing I woke up in a great mood, so I had some bagels and was on my way to the library, I opened the door and in front of me stood the brown haired girl from the pub. She slowly shut the door behind her locking it, she slowly inched forward, "it's a lovely morning Simon—well don't you think"? She asked this in a normal way, and I was surprised, her face was pale and she was quite small and skinny, but her brown locks circled her face, but leaving her ocean blue eyes for all to see. "So are you going to kill me too"? She quickly asked, looking at me with a smile. I gasped, "Why would I kill you"? I asked irritated, of course I wanted her dead 'she was my ticket to death', that's what she is. She eyed me slowly then rolled her eyes, "why did you kill him"? She asked calmly, twirling a chocolate brown lock of hair in her finger twisting it slowly. "How do you know my name"? I asked, rage filled my face and my head began to spin, 'she was toying with me'! I slowly came forward, "what do you want"? I screamed. She looked at me and her face went red, "I know who you are, and I know you killed your brother Adam, so if I were smart I would shut up and sit down". She screamed. "You know I could just go to the police, and tell them that you killed your brother". "It wouldn't be hard; I could just call them now". As she was babbling I was about to pass out, my body was throbbing and it felt like someone just punched me in the stomach. All my wind was knocked out of me and I fell to the ground, I was numb shocked to the core. She looked at me, and kicked me in the ribs. "Get up you little pussy". She screamed. I quickly jumped to my feet and grabbed her wrist. She looked at me and smiled, "well if you're going to do something then, do it"!! She screamed. I looked at her then shoved her back. She caught herself before she hit the ground, "she quickly jumped in my face and slapped me leaving my face, burning with friction. At that she left the room, slamming the door behind her. I just stood there, in shock fear trembled down my spine, and sweat balled on my forehead. 'How could of this have happened'? I asked myself on the verge of tears, 'how could I have been so blind'? I was nervous way too nervous. In the morning I would go to the pub and I would be careful and when I saw her I would follow her home, and at the perfect moment I would slash her throat. 'but I would have to stash the body' 'where would I stash the body'? I scanned my brain for these answers. 'Could I burn it?' No!' I could throw it in the river' No!, it might float up, 'I could tie a brick to the ankle, or 'possibly cut it up'. No way to messy hmmm . . . . I scanned my brain for the answers once again and nothing came forth. 'What would be the easiest way to dispose of a body'? Acid! That's it acid, it would just eat it whole and nothing would be left, 'but where would I get acid'? My brain was buzzing to the rim with this, I couldn't figure it out, and I had to dispose of the body, no doubt but how? 'I got it I would go to the soap shop and buy a few pounds of lye, and then I would dig a hole put the body in cover it with lye and watch it dissolve'. It was brilliant, I was brilliant!

Greenwich was a small town outside of the eastern part of London, and in the middle of that town was a small soap shop, and they were bound to have lye. So I took a bus over there and when I arrived I noticed all eyes were on me, scanning me from head to toe, an older lady came forth first, "sir can I help you"? She asked in a large voice. I sighed, "I'm here to pick of three pounds of lye". I said in a sincere voice tilting my head up as I said it. She smiled, "well you're in the perfect place to do so". She laughed. I looked at her uncomfortably, "well is there any way I can get some, I'm in a hurry". I said with a hint of frustration. She looked at me and sighed, "Well what are you using it for"? She asked in anger. I looked at her, "my boss is making soap or something". I muttered. She nodded, "well I'll have you know that I don't have that much right now, and tomorrow there will be a truck load coming in so you'll have to come back tomorrow". She said rolling her eyes. I looked at her, "well is there a hotel I can stay in until then"? She nodded, "yeah, down the street there is a motel called the Rolling Acre, you can stay their". With that she left. I just looked at my surroundings and sighed, it was a small town, not many stores and a few houses. I then walked over to the Rolling Acre, it was a homely place, and it was falling apart my room was very small, it had a small bathroom, a one person bed a small TV and a closet. I spent most of my time in the bar. I had a couple of drinks before some townies came over to me and started asking questions. Like 'where are you from'? Or 'what is your business here really'? I didn't say anything to them, frankly I ignored them, that is until a large fat man, came up to me and tried to push me back, but I quickly dodged him and left the bar, I slept ok that night, and woke to the beeping of a truck backing up. I quickly jumped out of the bed and went to the window, and in front of the soap shop a large black truck was parked and a fat little man was hauling what I thought was to be lye. I quickly ran down stairs to the truck and greeted the man, "sir, I was wondering if I could purchase three pounds of lye"? I asked smiling. He sighed and glanced at me, "oh, yeah boy of course, I cannot deny you that". He chuckled. Minutes later I was on a bus the bags of lye next to my feet. 'I have the lye, now I just have to find the girl' I thought. I was at my house in no time flat; I then unloaded the lye into my apartment and went to the pub. I stayed and watched for her for several hours but she never came around so I went home. Like usual I didn't sleep I could only think of killing that girl, she knew who I was and where I was staying and it bothered me that she hadn't called the cops. I went to the pub everyday for what it seemed was weeks and I never once saw her, I was drenched in fear, she was out there and I knew that any time she felt like it she could just go to the cops and tell them of my actions. But the thing is they would be curious of why she hadn't come to them sooner, and why she had waited so long to come forth with the truth. Or possibly they were waiting for her to vanish and that she already went to them and the second they found out she was gone they would come to me and lock me away. These horrid thoughts filled my head to the rim with agitation; I was so restless and sick to my stomach with fright. After another month or so I decided it would be best to just stay hidden, I never went out and I lived on the rations I had left, no one ever bothered me, that is until one day I had a sudden knock interrupted me, and in a split second I was at the door, and for several minutes I just stared at it, unsure of whether or not to open it, I opened it after tree more minutes, and in front of me stood two male officers, the first officer was tall and thin he had a mop of blonde hair, the second officer was short and fat, he had short neatly cut brown hair. I looked at them both, "may I help you officers"? I asked pleasantly. They exchanged looks and smiled, "Simon Lucre?" he asked politely. I nodded once, "yes that's me, why have you come"? I demanded. The blonde sighed, "I'm detective Williams and this is Officer Andrew "we need to ask you a couple of questions". He muttered, sighing at the end and scratching his head. I looked at them both, my legs froze and panic tremble in my body. "Why, what happened"? He looked at me, "do you happen to know a lady by the name of Anita Ancline, she is a middle aged woman, and she's tall and has brown hair, and has off grey eyes". As he was muttering I was in shock, they had me, I screwed up and now they would lock me away, forever. As he finished the exact portrayal of Anita I was numb. I quickly looked at the officer's, detective Williams was still talking but I didn't hear anything, the world was mute and then it all came crashing in. "son, are you ok"? He asked worried. I looked at him, "I'm fine, what was your question"? He sighed, "Do you know Anita Ancline, oh and I've come to believe that she was your land lady"? He finished. "Yes she is my land lady, but I haven't seen her in a great time. I said lying through my teeth. The officer sighed and muttered something to the other officer, "she's your land lady how is it that you haven't seen her, son where were you on Friday the sixth"? He asked sternly, taking a pen and pad from his pocket, I looked at them both and smiled. "I was at home of course". I said boldly. He twitched his nose and looked at me, "says here you were at the local pub on the sixth". He muttered staring straight through me. "I might have gone to the pub, I'm not sure, why are you asking me"? I asked in a hushed voice. He looked at me, "son, we don't want any trouble, we would just like to know if you had any information on the murder of Anita Ancline, now it says here that you, went to Luv`ancle Tint on march 8, may I ask why you went"? He questioned bitterly. I sighed, "I was going to see my uncle". I lied. The officer smiled, "says here you bought three pounds of lye, now tell me son if you went there to see our uncle then why did you buy lye"? He asked. Sweat balled on my forehead and I was nervous, too nervous. "I was making soap, now I don't see what this has to do with the death of Anita". I replied. He smiled, "son have you ever seen this?" he asked this as he pulled out a small plastic bag which held my silver pocket knife. I gasped, "No that's not mine". I said in outrage. The officer once again smiled, "a couple of officers found this by the dumpster, where they also found Anita's body; we will have fingerprints next week". He said in a threatening voice. "So what does this have to do with me"? I asked. "Well son, I'm just doing my job". He muttered. I blinked, "well I'm sorry but I don't have any further information for you, so you should be going now". I said in mono tone, the officer's looked at me in shock, "sure son, but we will be keeping a close eye on you". The brown haired officer said. I smiled, "why would you be doing that, am I a suspect"? I asked surprised. A smirk filled his face "possibly yes and possibly no". He tipped his hat and they left. 'I was a suspect, they knew who I was' I was in a complete overload of fear when they left, 'the girl from the bar, she must have told them, that was all, but the knife that was my knife' I could disappear, I had enough money, I could just up and leave, I had no worries, and no one really knew me, but the girl and those cops, they knew me, and I was in so much danger being here so I would have to leave, it was my only option, I would hide away in the country for a while and once this all cleared away I would come back, and the nice thing was that no one would notice. That night I went to the pub and in the corner of the bar was that girl, I crept into the pub without her noticing and when she left, which was about eleven o' clock I followed her home, she was about an inch away from her door when I hit her over the head with a rock. I stood over her as she drew the last breath, 'how could I get her home'? I asked myself. That night I stashed the body in the trunk of her car and to my surprise the keys were in the ignition so I drove to my house and grabbed a shovel the lye and several sheets. I found a perfect place to dig a hole, the location was behind a large near burnt down barn, and I quickly began to dig a hole, I then wrapped the body in sheets and threw it into the hole. I then as planned dumped all the lye on top and filled in the hole. That night I packed my stuff and hit the high road, I traveled to the plains, and camped out for several years in an old abandoned barn, I grew thinner and thinner, my face was covered in a ton of hair and I smelt terrible, the air around me was cold and I nearly froze to death one night. I must have lived in that barn for two or three years, and as planned no one ever came looking for me, I lived off of the rats that inhabited the rafters and decaying hay and I drank the rain runoff from the metal tin roof. Never once did I sleep, I was too scared to close my eyes, and far too cold to even think about it. When I finally left the barn I had nothing I came as I went empty handed, only the rags on my back. The sight of the pedestrians made me immediately sick, and the awful stench of the poor dying on the streets made me gag. I just stood there at the corner of the street, I had no money and no home, and I was a homeless mangy person and frankly a pathetic one at that. From there I lived in a small old abandoned half burnt down house, I once again survived on the rodents that dwelled there. I suppose I can't say I was broke I had money, but it was in the old apartment house I had time age, it was at least thirty dollars wrapped in a wash cloth neatly tucked under the floor boards in the kitchen. I just wasn't sure how I was able to even retrieve it, one I would have to find my way back there and I doubted it was vacant, and if it was it would be considerably easy to gather my left over money, if not I imagined it would be quite impossible. I slept for the first night in what it seemed years; it wasn't a soundless sleep or even a warm one but I slept and that was all that mattered. When I woke I walked the streets for hours, nothing was where it had been when I was a citizen, so I found it quite hard to find the apartments, and when I did, I was shocked to find out it was now a whore house called Lady Lord, I was unsure of how to approach it, I slowly walked in the doors and was immediately accompanied by a large fat man with a chin full of red hair. "Morning sunny, how may I help ya today"? He asked in a chipper way. I smiled "I use to live here, and I was wondering if I could see my old room real fast"? I asked half hoping he would say yes. He smiled and rubbed his hairy chin, "I'll make ya a deal if ya take one of these lovely girls up you can go see all the rooms". He laughed. "Rose"!! he screamed and seconds later a blonde woman walked in she wore a short crimson dress white lace sewn around the edges she was bare footed and I instantly felt hot in my face, "rose take this man up and show him a grand time". He smiled looking at me. The woman named rose slowly grasped my hand and pulled me up the fleet of stairs, "madam might I ask you a question"? I asked in a soothing voice. She quickly turned and looked at me, "my, oh my, what a gentleman, ask any thing and call me rose". She sputtered. I sighed, "is their anyway I can bathe and clean up"? I asked. She smiled, "I'll make you a deal, I'll let ya clean yourself, but ya can't ever tell Mr. Matson's". She giggled. "Might I also tell you something"? I asked. She smiled, "what is it cutie"? She laughed. "I've never done anything of this sort before". I choked. She quickly stopped walking, and turned towards me, "are you serious"? She gasped. I nodded, "is that weird"? I questioned. She quickly pulled me closer to her and she kissed my cheek, "oh you little baby, I'll take care of you". She cooed. When we entered the room, she quickly pushed me on the bed, "ok now take your clothes off and I'll be back in a few". She ordered this as she went into the bathroom. I did as she said, and never before did I feel the urge I had now, and I wasn't even sure what I was urging for. As said she was out of the bathroom in seconds, she was stark naked and she was beautiful, she had ivory skin and the loveliest body, she slowly inched forward, and when she reached the bed, she climbed on top of me, she twisted my hair in her fingers and kissed my lips, I don't think I can put the episode into words but I will try it was like nothing I had ever felt before and it felt like I had fed my body what it had been longing for. I left the room after I cleaned myself and cut my hair, I still wore the rags, I slowly went to my old room which to no surprise looked like the other room just an open area with a bed and a bathroom, I slowly went to where my kitchen use to lye, I kneeled down and traced the boards with my fingers, I knew that the board that held my money wasn't flush to the ground so it wasn't long before I found it and collected my money. I paid the boss ten cents for the experience, and he smiled and said that I was welcomed anytime. I then went to the Tom and Jerry's, it was a small suite and hat shop, there I purchased a suite a top hat and a silk cape, it totaled up to one dollar. And from their I looked like the average London citizen, I needed a job though and a house so I immediately went to the market and asked for a job, I was hired by a tall slender man with the most piercing of eyes he gave me a job, which consisted of loading and unloading trucks. I made two dollars a day and that was plenty enough for lodging and food, I rented a small apartment, which held a small bed and a bath. It was enough, I now had a job and a home and it seemed I was back to where I had originally begun. My job was only a few blocks away from my apartment so I could easily walk there. I went back to the Lady Lord's about every other day, though I spent most of the hours with rose, and then one day I decided to take her out to the finest restraint in all of London, the Capricorn Diner. We talked about really nothing and when we were done with dinner we went for a stroll in the park. I bought her some red roses and then brought her back to the Lady Lord's. I'd never once felt as invincible as when I was with rose, she was beautiful and hard working, she was the one, and so I hoped she would soon become more. When I arrived at the apartments I was accompanied by a detective, he was tall and slender and had a mop of untrimmed blonde hair; upon his head sat a bowler hat and he wore a long brown trench coat, I eyed him curiously. He smiled when he came forth, "Son I'm Detective Camborne, and I was wondering if I could ask you a couple of questions"? He asked in a demanding way. Once again my body filled with nervousness. I nodded, "what may I help you with"? I asked politely. He smiled, "just yesterday there was a horrid murder in the market, and several people have told me that you have been working there so I was wondering if you have seen this man"? He asked as he pulled out a crinkled paper with an illustration on it of a bald man with glasses. I shook my head, "no sir I haven't seen that man, but if I do I will contact you". I said slowly. He nodded and started to walk away but turned and looked at me, "have we met before young man"? He asked in an uneasy way. Quickly gazed at him, "no, not that I remember". I said lying, because the man in front of me was the same man that came to me and asked me questions about the sudden death of Anta Ancline. I was drenched in fear, and in that second I was hoping that his eyes would betray him. He sighed, "Well if you have any information about this man, contact me immediately". He instructed. I nodded and slowly walked away, out of the corner of my eye I saw him watching me with curiosity as I walked down the cobblestone streets. I knew deep inside of me he knew who I was, and if I screwed up once he would find me and take me away. Went to work that day and stayed later than usual, which consulted into me making more money, I then went to the Lady Lord's and asked for Rose, but was told that she was busy at the moment and that if I waited she would be available in no time flat. I didn't stay that time I just went home and immediately went to bed, I slept well that night and when I woke I went straight to work and after went to the Lady Lord's to see Rose, I once again took her out and bought her some flowers and after we just sat on a bench in the park, I caressed her hands in mine and whispered sweet things into her ear, as the sun began to go down, we gradually started on our way back to the Lady Lord's, I asked her as we approached the entrance if she lived here, she sighed and smiled, "no Simon I only work here, I live about six blocks down I just have to gather a few items and then I'll go home, why do you ask"? She questioned. I quickly pulled her into my arms, "well I wanted to actually walk you home tonight, if that's ok". I muttered. Her eyes grew wide and a radiant smile filled her lips, "I would love that Simon, you're such a gentleman". She laughed and kissed my forehead. I quickly took her by the hand and I took her home. Her house was an apartment like mine but she lived on the lower part I stopped at the door. She looked at me, "well you can come in if you'd like". She said smiling. She showed me around her house, first her bedroom; she had a twin bed and a large dresser with a couple of coffee tables. Her bathroom was small like mine, but she had a kitchen and a living area. After the tour she pulled me into the bedroom and we made love for several hours. I stayed the night with her and in the morning I made her some eggs and toast. I left before she woke, immediately went home and changed into my work uniform and then went to work. After work I didn't go home or to see rose I went to the bar, and as you can imagine it was the same old Pub. I arrived rather quickly after work I needed a drink. I ordered a couple of whisky's and just sat at the counter in harmony, that is until the detective showed up, he sat down next to me and ordered the same as me. I slowly sipped my whisky and tried not to notice that he was beside me, and then out of the blue he looked at me and smiled. "How are you son"? He asked in a mono tone. I glanced at him out of the corner of my eye, "oh I'm great, and you sir"? I asked quietly. He smiled and looked at me from top to bottom, "oh you're the young man from the market". He said loudly. I nodded, "yes sir that's me". I said, boldly. He smiled and finished his drink, "you know I never got your name son, how about it who are ya"? He asked. I looked at him nervously, "oh I'm um . . . . My name is Louis". I said quietly. He nodded and ordered another shot. I was nervous too nervous, and for a second I thought that it was actually pouring off of me. He looked at me once more, "I know you, I just don't remember where from". He said scratching his head. I sighed, "Well detective it was nice to see you again, but I must be on my way". I said then quickly stood up and put my coat on, he looked at me, "you know son, and I have to go also so how about we walk together"? He asked, but in a way demanded. I smiled and nodded, "that would be splendid". I lied. He nodded and followed me out. I noticed as he watched me every second while we walked, I looked at him "so detective how long have you worked for the government"? I asked looking down. He eyed me quickly, "oh for about ten to twenty years". "What about you Louis, how long have you been in London"? I knew by then that he was finally catching on. I looked at him rather quickly, "oh I'd say for about a year or so". I lied once more. He nodded. "Well this is me". He said pointing to a large white house. I nodded. "Well, bye then". I said slowly and as I was about to turn the corner, he called me back. "Louis, what's your last name"? He asked in suspicion. I looked at him, "Mc. Gomery, Louis Mc. Gomery". I spewed out. He nodded and went inside. I slowly walked away again, he had me, it didn't matter if I changed my name, and he knew who I was, and in no time flat he would arrest me and never let me go. I immediately went home after that, I didn't know what to do, it seemed no matter how long I waited, or how long I vanished, that man would find me. The only option I had was to kill him, and I doubted it would be that simple or even easy. The next day I immediately went to see rose, only to find that she hadn't bothered to show up. At that I went to her apartment, I knocked several times but she never answered so I went in, I found her still in bed, I slowly walked over to the bed and leaned down and kissed her forehead, I must have frightened her because she lashed out at me, causing me to fall and hit my head on the dresser, she was at my side by then planting sorry kisses all over my face. I quickly pulled her down beside me, "good morning sexy". I smiled. She looked into my eyes for several seconds, "you scared me, and how is it that you got in"? She asked in a surprised voice. I kissed her quickly but rather softly, your door was open and I knocked several times. She smiled, you're a good man Simon, and I looked at her "I'm going to leave the country for a while so I was wondering if you would like to come" she looked at me quickly, "why are you leaving? She asked in worry. I smiled, "no real reason". I said with a laugh. She smiled, "where would you go"? She asked. I smiled and kissed her hand, "I'm not sure yet, possibly America". I said with excitement. She smiled, "oh Simon, you should go to America, what a beautiful place". She gasped. I smiled, "then not me but you and I". She looked at me, "Simon I can't just go running off with you, I have a home and a job besides why would I want to go to America when I have a life here"? I looked at her, "America has so many options for a new life, rose I love you and if you don't come with me then I will not be". I said in sadness. She lifted my chin and kissed me softly, "Simon I love you to but!" I cut her off, "have dinner with me tomorrow night at dusk meet me at the Finoaut". I said smiling. She stood up and pulled me up also, "Simon why are you doing this"? She asked in desperation. I kissed her forehead, "because Rose I love you, when I saw you for the first time I felt a urging inside of me, don't you see, that urging was you". I said slowly. She looked up at me tears rolling down her red cheeks, "oh Simon you're so sweet, yes I'll meet you tomorrow. She laughed. I quickly pulled her close and kissed her head then went home. I slept well that night and in the morning didn't go to work instead I went to the jewelers and bought a ring, there were so many and it was hard to find one that I thought she would adore, after about ten minutes I found a silver ring with a ruby an top it was perfect and I knew she would love it, after that I went home and cleaned the house, I stopped by the Lady Lord's and saw rose, she was just sitting on the bed when I found her, "I bought you something". I said cheerfully. She looked at me with a smile, "what is it"? She begged. I sighed, "You'll have to wait until tonight to find out". I said smiling. She slightly shoved me and then jumped on me, "I'll hold you down forever if you don't tell me". She threatened. I smiled, "I'm not stopping you, so go ahead". I laughed. She kissed my head, "you're such a butt head". She teased. I meet her at the restraint and when I saw her I nearly choked, she was wearing a blood red gown, and for a moment it looked as if she were wearing a dress of rose petals. I smiled and took her to her seat. We ordered some red wine and just sat and stared at each other. "So Simon, what is this surprise you've for me"? She asked eagerly. I smiled and slowly took the box with the ring out of my pocket and slipped it into her hands. Her eyes widened and a radiant smile masked her glowing face, "oh Simon". She gasped then slowly opened it. I then took the ring and went down on one knee, "rose, my love will you marry me"? I asked. She was in tears by then her face red and swollen, "oh Simon, yes, yes I'll marry you". At that I slipped the ring onto her finger, by then she was in my arms and was crying. I noticed as all eyes were on us, which ended in a loud applause. I smiled and kissed her gently, "Oh congratulations, Louis ". I voice said, I turned around to see the detective behind me. "Oh Louis she is glowing with beauty". By then rose was eying me quite frequently. She smiled at him, and sighed, "Well it's late detective and we must be on our way". She said loudly. He looked at her in a curious way, "oh my lady, call me William". He replied in haste. I smiled at rose and took her by the hand, "ok love let's go before it gets too dark". I said politely. Rose was still staring at me and a frown had completely covered her face. William's by then was staring at me in a cruel way, "possibly I can walk the newlywed's home; it would be a polite thing to do". He suggested. Rose smiled, "oh what a lovely thing to do William's but I think we can manage". She said cunningly. He smiled and rubbed his mustache. "Well ok then, have a wonderful night". He yelled as we went out the door. Rose turned towards me as we left the place, "Louis huh, who are you really"? She asked. I sighed "rose my name is Simon and before you I was in trouble, so when that detective asked me my name I lied, because I didn't want to hurt you". I said pleading. She looked at me in anger, "well I'll have you know Simon, or Louis or whoever the hell you are, if this marriage thing is going to work, you must tell me what happened why you are in trouble and I don't want any secrets . . . do you understand me?". She screamed bitterly. I smiled, "rose, I've done some terrible things in my life so far, and I don't think that telling you would better us". I said smiling. She turned and looked at me, "there will be no secrets Simon, I want to trust you and I want us to be happy, but if you lie to me or hide things I promise we won't last". She threatened. I nodded, "ok rose, but before I shine the light on these awful sins, I want you to not judge me". I said in a weary tone. She looked at me in curiosity, "Simon you act as if you've killed someone, but no I will ever judge you". She said smiling. I sighed, "When I was younger I lived with my parents and my little brother Adam, see Adam and I hated each other, or I hated him, you see before him I had a family and my parents paid attention to me and bought me things and made me happy, but the minute when Adam appeared everything around me vanished, no more happiness and no more love, my parents were cold to me, and when I tried to love them they pushed me away. So I made a plan to hurt Adam, so that my parents could see, that I was still there. And when I put the plan into action, they sent me away to my aunt she wasn't any better she was insane and when I stayed with her she would hurt me badly. So I put an end to her, after that I moved here I found Adam then and when I did I killed him also". I noticed that as I was saying this we had stopped walking, and she just stood beside me mouth open, eyes round and wide, "oh Simon, that's horrid, and why would you kill them"? She begged. I looked at her in fury, "they took everything I had ever had, they made me cold and filled with hate, it's their fault that I'm the way that I am". I screamed. She looked at me in pity, "Simon the past is the past and you must move on, just don't think about it, those were awful things you did, but they are over and you had no idea of what you were doing, move on". She said slowly. I quickly pulled her in close to me, "I love you rose, and I will never stop". I said as I kissed her lips. She kissed back and smiled, "I love you also and I too will never stop". She said in a whisper. We started to walk again and I held her hand tight, "so what about you rose, what's your story"? I asked. She smiled, "it isn't much, my mother died when I was young and my father left me to my uncle, I lived with him and went to school here in London, after that I decided it was time to start my own life, I suppose things didn't go the right way, because I ended up here as a whore, and when I was about to give up I found you". She finished. I smiled, "rose, I don't want you to work there any longer, I want you to be mine and only mine". She smiled, "actually I was going to quit tomorrow, I hate it there and what I do is low". She said sighing. I smiled, "well after tonight you're a new woman, a whole different person". I smiled. She looked at me, "Simon a ring doesn't change a person, I'm the same person married or not". She laughed she sighed and looked at me "so Simon where are we going"? She asked. I looked at her, "home". I said shortly. She nudged me in the ribs, "you said that you wanted to travel". She reminded. "Oh travel, I was thinking that we should go to America and start new and fresh". I said. She smiled, "oh America that would be wonderful". She gasped. I smiled and kissed her hand. "You know that if we do, you'd have to leave everything behind". I said reminding her. She sighed and squeezed my hand "I love you that's all that matters". She said in a low whisper. She looked at me, "Simon, will you promise me something"? She asked through clenched teeth. I nodded "anything". I said pulling her close to me. "Promise me that you will never hurt anyone again". She said quickly. I looked at her shocked, "hurt how"? I asked in a mono tone. "Like kill Simon, promise me that you won't ever kill again". She sputtered. I looked at her quickly and stopped walking, "rose, are you scared of me"? I asked surprised. She returned my look with a short one, "no, I'm not scared of you, and I don't intend to be, I just want us to have a wonderful life together have children someday and grow old together, that's all". She said rather slowly. I looked at her shocked, "you want to have kids"? I asked doubtingly. She nodded, "oh of course I want kids; a boy and a girl". She laughed. I smiled, "that would be truly amazing". I said in shyness. She looked at me, "so who is moving in with whom"? She asked in an awkward way. "What do you mean"? I asked staring at her. "Well when someone gets engaged to another, one of them moves in with the other". She said in a smirk. "Well which do you prefer"? I asked in a rush. "Well it would seem that I have the better house of us two so you should stay with me". She replied laughing. I smiled, "well that won't be that hard, and I hardly have any belongings, just some clothes and some hats". I said slowly. She nodded. By then we were at her door; she smiled and unlocked it, then quickly pulled me in. "I owe you a thank you". She laughed quickly taking down her hair. We didn't really have a ceremony for a wedding we just thought of it as that from the beginning of the night that we were married. She then pulled me into the room, I then slowly and softly unbuttoned her dress, I watched as it fell down to her feet surrounding her like a pool of water. She turned towards me and placed her hands on my chest, then slowly ran her fingers down to the rim of my pants. She then slowly unbuttoned them and at the last one I nearly collapsed in want. She then pulled my shirt off. We were on the bed by then, her naked body sprawled across the white silk sheets; she was a goddess, a radiant star, my star now and forever. I then slowly lye on top of her, resulting into us rolling over each other that is until she was on top, at that I slowly traced her soft lips with my fingers tracing all the way down to her thigh, I caressed her gently and kissed her with a tinge of force. She liked it though, she quickly kissed me back biting my bottom lip, it bled a little and I noticed that it tasted of salt and had a thick texture. I smiled and bit her neck a little not enough to make it bleed but enough to turn her on, she screamed in pleasure and wrestled me down on the bed, she held my hands down on the bed and stared into my eyes, "you have the sexiest o eyes". She said soundly. I looked at her, "how so"? I asked. She shrugged her shoulders, "I'm not sure but they always seem to change colors, brown to a light blue or a silvery gray, they fascinate me, you fascinate me". She said as a large smile danced across her face. I rolled my eyes, "you're a dork, and I think it's about time that I win this fight". I said in laughter then quickly pulled her underneath me, "your weak, and to be honest it's sexy". I said while kissing her stomach. She laughed and tried to get away, "stop that tickles, Simon stop". She laughed. But I didn't stop I just watched as she tried to get free. She quickly stopped laughing, "This isn't fair, you know"! She choked out. I looked at her quickly, "how so?" she smiled, "because you're stronger than me, and frankly you've to let me win to". She said slowly catching her breath as she said it. "Are you whining"? I teased. She made a silly face, "no me whining, ha I would never". She said quickly. I smiled, "well it sounds like you are". I mumbled in a sarcastic voice. She flashed me a half angry look, "Simon look"! She screamed staring at the doorway; I quickly turned to look, resulting into her rolling on top of me. "Now tell me who is weak"? She laughed. I looked back at her, "that doesn't count, you cheated". I moaned. She smiled, "are you whining, because it sounds like it to me"? She said sarcastically. I sighed, "ok, ok you win but only because I let you"! I said laughing. She rolled her eyes, "oh please, you're just saying that because you lost". She replied. The night seemed to go by rather quickly, and in the morning I woke to the smell of warm food and several loud noises. I sprang out of bed and walked into the kitchen, rose was stark naked in the kitchen making breakfast, she smiled when she saw me, "morning sexy, I made you breakfast". She said. I looked at her from head to toe, and then quickly pulled her into me kissing her softly. She smiled, "well good morning to you too". She said in a laugh. "Rose, you do know that you are naked while making breakfast". I said laughing. She nodded, "yes and your point is"? She asked as she served me up an egg some bacon and few pieces of toast on a plate. She then slowly and gently set it down in front of me. I sighed, "well I don't have a problem with it I love your body, I just think you should be carefull because you could possibly get burned". I said then took a bite of a piece of bacon. She smiled, "are you going to work today"? She asked suddenly. I nodded, "yeah I start at seven ten". She smiled, "just enough time for me to man handle you". She said quickly. I smiled and finished my food. We quickly made love and after I went to work, but not without a kiss from rose. I had a wonderful day, and several random people congratulated me and rose. I went home earlier that day and when I arrived at roses, she wasn't there, so I took a nap. I woke to the close of the door, "Simon, are you home"? Rose called from the kitchen, I quickly jumped up and went into the kitchen, and she smiled when she saw me, "your home early" she said surprised. I sighed, "Well how was your day lovely"? I asked. She smiled, "well I just quit my job, Mr. Matson wasn't very happy, and I bought some flowers" she lifted up a boutique of purples, blues, whites and red roses, I smiled, "they are lovely but not as lovely as you". I said walking towards her. I watched as her cheeks lit up, "and you, how was your day"? She asked in a sweet voice. "It was ok; I mean there wasn't that much business". I muttered. She smiled and was putting the flowers in a vase on the table. She flashed me a smirk, and then scratched her head. "So what would you like for dinner"? She asked. I looked at her, "I'm not sure, how about cake"? I asked in hope. She rolled her eyes, "cake is not a dinner food". She replied. I sighed, "Ok how about pie"? I teased. She quickly reached out and punched me in the shoulder, I laughed at that and smiled. "Simon I mean real food, not sweets, so what will it be"? She demanded. "Ok what about lasagna"? I asked. Her eyes lit up, "that sounds wonderful, and so have you heard or had any sightings of that detective William's"? She asked. "no and I hope it stays that way, that man is only out for one thing and that's to put me away". I said bitterly. She looked at me curiously, "how could he even put you away, you were young when you did all that". She said in frustration. She then looked at me suddenly, "Simon, what else did you do did you kill any one that you didn't tell me about"? She asked in a low voice. I looked at her quickly, "there was someone else, her name was Anita Ancline, she was my landlady, and she threatened to kick me out". I said in a whisper. She looked at me frustrated. "Why didn't you tell me about her Simon I thought we agreed to no secrets"? She said in a hurt voice. I sighed, "Rose I'm sorry I hid that from you". I said slowly. She sighed, "Did anyone see you Simon when you killed any of those people did anyone at all"? She asked in an eager tone. I nodded, "yes there was this girl, I don't know who she is, but I know that she hasn't told the police about me". I said in satisfaction. She sighed, "And how is it you can be so calm about that, Simon she could just go tell them, or maybe she already has and they are just waiting for you to kill again". She said bitterly. I looked at her shocked, "well I don't know where she is, and I don't intend to kill again, why is this so important to you"? I asked in frustration. She was crying by then, "I can't lose you Simon, you're everything to me." I didn't sleep that night I was in panic, I knew that in reality I was in trouble, and for a moment I wanted to kill again, it made me feel so strong and capable, and that's when I decided it was time to do so, I knew that I couldn't hold my sinful urges any longer and if I did it would result into me killing rose. I dreamt about my next victim, and what joy it would bring me, I just lye their all night I softly traced rose's curves with my pointer finger kissing her softly. I missed work the next day on purpose, but I still went out, I scanned the crowds all day for that special next victim, but none of them made me tick inside. I then went to the bar and had a couple of drinks, and from across the bar stood that girl. I suddenly choked on my tongue, which resulted into me gasping for air. I slowly approached her from behind; she quickly turned towards me and gasped, "Simon"? She screamed in surprise. I grinned, "So how are you" . . . I paused "I never got your name miss". I said quickly. She looked at me worried, "what do you want with me Simon"? She asked in a whisper. I smiled, "your name miss". I said in excitement. She quickly drew in a breath, "veronica". She replied in a low voice. I smiled, "would you like to talk somewhere else"? I asked. Her eyes widened, "no stay away from me". She screamed and ran out of the bar. I laughed as the door slammed shut; all eyes were on me by then, but only for a second. I left the bar after she left I followed her then feet away; I lurked behind her I watched as she went inside a yellow trailer house. I went home after I followed her there, and to my surprise rose wasn't home. She came home about two hours after I came home, and in her hands were several paper bags, "oh hi love I went food sopping, so what do you want for dinner tonight, we can have chicken stake, or spaghetti or possibly meat loaf, whatever you want". She said smiling. I sighed, "Honestly I'm not hungry". I said in a sigh. She smiled, "ok then, why don't you go lie down, I'll be there in a couple of seconds". She said with a smile.

I fell asleep rather quickly that night, I was exhausted and I dreamt the same dream, about the next victim I was to kill. Rose was cuddled up to me and she smelt of flowers, sweet and delicious. I woke up around three in the morning and for several minutes I just stared at rose, she was angelic when she slept. I then quickly changed into some pants and a shirt and went out, I went to that yellow trailer house, I slowly stood at the door and carefully twisted the knob, the door wasn't locked so you can only imagine what joy I was in when it easily opened, I sneaked inside and went straight to the bedroom, and in the middle of the bed lye Victoria sound asleep, I had never killed someone in their sleep before so I hoped it would be easy, and less noisy. I then slowly drew my knife from my pocket, I then inched forward to where I was at the side of the bed, I lifted the knife over her chest and with one powerful thrust I stabbed her in the heart, she didn't even make a noise, and for that I was thankful. I watched as blood poured from her lips onto her white blankets, by then my gloves were soaked so I quickly took them off and set them down on the bed stand, and for a moment I thought I was dreaming, I felt incredible, alive and fearless. I left her there and slowly went home, rose was still asleep so I quickly took a bath and changed my clothing, and I threw away the knife in a dumpster on the way. That's when I noticed that I had forgotten my gloves, my head started to buzz and I felt sick extremely sick, I fell to my knees and my head had exploded into a headache, it throbbed and my body was tense. I went straight to bed then and I slept ok. Rose was up before me, I slowly got up and in the bathroom was rose, her head over the toilet. I quickly kneeled down beside her and patted her back, "rose what's wrong, are you ok"? I begged. She lifted her head up and looked at me, "I think there is something wrong with me". She cried. I sighed, "I'm going to take you to the clinic today rose, when did you start throwing up"? I asked. She blinked, "I'm not sure, every morning since last week". She said in a whisper. I nodded, "rose clean up and get dressed, were going to the clinic". I ordered. She slowly stood up and went to change. We were at the clinic in minutes, a female doctor came in and ran a few tests, and she came back with a wide smile. "Well I have great news, you're pregnant". She laughed. I looked at rose who was now wide eyed and gasping, she looked at me with a large smile, "Simon, were having a baby". She screamed in happiness. I smiled, "rose that's wonderful". I said slowly. She quickly looked at me, "Simon what's wrong, are you not happy with the news"? She asked bitterly. I quickly looked at her, "of course I'm happy, were having a baby rose". I said stunned with her stupid question. She smiled, "well doctor am I free to go"? She asked in a sweet voice the doctor nodded and smiled, "free to go". St that she left the room. We went home after that and just sat on the couch, her hands in mine and her head on my shoulder, "Simon, are you happy that were having a baby"? She asked again. I looked at her, by then I was a little frustrated, "why do you keep asking me that, yes I'm happy, I'm happy ok". I barked loudly. Her eyes went wide and she inched away from me, "what is you damn problem Simon, I'm asking because you don't seem that happy"? She screamed her face turning a shade of red. I looked at her in anger, "you know what rose, and frankly I just want to be left alone right now". I yelled. She quickly stood up and left the room slamming the bedroom door behind her. I just sat there in frustration, honestly I wasn't ready for a kid, I still had a life to live and with a kid I would never be able to do the things I wanted to do, and not only that it would cost a fortune to provide for it, all my hard earned money would immediately go to a crib and diapers and clothes and food. I was in a panic still from last night to, how could I have been so dumb? I went to work as usual that day without a word to rose when I left. I acted normal until that detective found me. "Morning, Simon lucre" He said in anger. I was shocked a little. He came closer and smiled, "so Simon, how long did you actually think that you could fool me, I'm not a stupid man Simon so where were you last night Simon"? He asked in suspicion. I smiled, "I was at home detective". I said boldly. He sighed, "Simon, don't lie to me, I found these at the crime scene". He said as he pulled out a plastic bag holding my blood coated gloves. My eyes widened. "Simon you listen to me, by the end of the day I will have fingerprints and the person who did it". He said in a threatening tone. I smiled at him, "well you do that, I have to get back to work". I said sarcastically he smiled at me and patted my shoulder, "I have a feeling that I might be seeing you real soon". He said then slowly walked away from me. I went home in a rush after that. I quickly opened the door and in the living room stood the detective and rose, she gave me a hateful look as I entered and the detective smiled at me as I entered also. He left seconds later and I felt a large tension between rose and I, "I can explain rose". I said quickly. Her eyes were red and filed with hate, "you bastard, how could you? You said you would never do it again, and how dare you come here, I don't forgive you Simon, and frankly right now I don't like you". She said in tears. I sighed, "Rose we can leave right now, we can escape to America right now". I said slowly. She sighed, "Simon it's too late, they are coming for you, and they know you did it". She said looking at the floor. I looked at her angrily, "well I'm leaving rose, and I don't care what you say, I'm not going to jail rose so if you want to stay then stay, if not come with me". I pleaded. She wiped her eyes, "ok Simon I'll go with you, but we have to leave right now Simon I mean right now". She informed. We were on the train in no time flat; we brought nothing. We boarded the train and sat next to each other.

She didn't once look at me, she avoided my eyes and it made me sick to my stomach. "Rose forgive me, I can't go on if you don't forgive me, please rose". I begged. She lifted her eyes to mine and jumped into my arms, "oh Simon I just don't want us to live like this, and you're a fugitive now Simon and I helped you so I'm just as bad". She cried. I held her tight and planted kisses all over her face, "rose once we are to America we can start over, we can become two different people". I said in a reassuring voice. She sighed, "Simon I don't want to be anyone else, and I don't want to have to change Simon, and I just want to live a normal life". She said slowly. I looked at her then and inside of me I wanted to be free of her and her wretched plan, she annoyed me and I wanted so badly to end her. I quickly put on a smile and rubbed her cheek, "I never said you had to come along rose, you could have just stayed". I said coolly. She looked at me in rage, "you are such an ass Simon, first you want me to come and now you act like you can't stand me". She screamed. I looked at her and slowly pushed her away, "that's because all you do is whine, you act like a child rose, just grow up already". I blurted out loud. She quickly stood up, "fuck you Simon, and don't you call me a child, this is your fault, all of this you killed that woman and now look at us". "I warned you Simon, I told you what would happen, and you ignored me, and because of it look at where we are". She screamed. I was in her face by then, and I so badly wanted to just punch her, she flashed me a warning look, "go ahead Simon I know you want to, just do it hit me come on you chicken". She screamed. I quickly pushed her away from me and left her; I went to the bar in the train and ordered several shots. After the fifth one I decided to go back to rose, she was asleep on the bench, and when I saw her I nearly broke down in tears, I loved her no doubt, but at times I wanted her gone. I slowly sat down beside her and slid my fingers through her hair, when she saw me she started crying I pulled her into me and kissed her forehead, "rose I'm sorry I said all that, I didn't mean it, I love you rose and I always will". I reassured. She wiped her eyes and looked at me, "I'm sorry to Simon, I'm just so nervous, I don't want you to go, and I love you so much". She cried. I lifted her face up to mine and kissed her softly, "Rose will you do something for me"? I asked in desperation. She looked at me and nodded, "will you forget about what happened and never bring it up again"? I asked. She smiled, "yes I promise". She said softly.

Chapter 6

In America

We arrived in America after three days, and when we got there, we both started looking for a house and work, we found a small mediocre house, and it had the normal two bedrooms a bath a kitchen and a living room. She started working at the market and I got a job at the butcher shop. As months passed rose's belly started to grow, at times I could feel the kick of the baby inside, and it brought such joy to me. She eventually stopped working because she became too exhausted at times to do any more. I on the other hand stayed working, at the last month of her pregnancy I finally could afford a crib and all the baby things that we needed. I was at work when I got the call, rose was rushed to the hospital by the neighbor, she was in labor when I arrived I just stood at her side holding her hand tight, "push"! The nurse, Screamed. Rose just stared at me in horror, "I am pushing"! She screamed back. Then in an instant a tiny scream filled the room, the nurse slowly cleaned the baby off and gave it to rose, "it's a girl rose". She congratulated, but all of a sudden rose let out another scream, the nurse quickly took the baby away, "twins doctor, push rose push"! She screamed. Rose pushed one last time and out came another scream. The nurse did the same and then gave it to Rose, "a boy and a girl". She said in a proud way. Rose looked at me, "Simon we had twins". She said through tears. I smiled and took the boy into my arms he was beautiful, the loveliest baby I had ever seen. "What should we name him"? I asked. She smiled, "what about Edgar"? She asked. I nodded, "Edgar, what a beautiful name". I said slowly. She smiled, "and this one, how about Edith"? She asked. I stayed with rose, that night and cradled the twins in my arms, and sang them a lullaby. They were angles, my angles, Edith and Edgar I said slowly almost in a whisper. Rose and I were able to go home the next day, the twins had to stay a few more day in the hospital, so I went out and bought another crib, and more baby things. Rose said that she would breast feed them, so I wouldn't have to buy formula for them. When we finally were able to bring them home, I immediately started working again. Rose spent every waking hour with the twins; we hardly slept at all, the constant cry of the twins kept us up all night. And I was always exhausted by the end of the day. It wasn't long before they were out of diapers and walking about, I remember coming home after work one day and I the middle of the carpet sat the twins both saying momma and dada, at the same time. I smiled when I saw this and quickly pulled them both into my arms, and then started tickling them. Rose was standing by the kitchen table with a beautiful smile displayed across her face. I slowly put them down and pulled rose towards me, "look at them love, they are so beautiful". I said while kissing her cheek, she smiled and hugged me quickly. "Oh Simon we have a wonderful family, look at the kids they are so happy". She cried. I kissed her lips and squeezed her tight, "I love you rose and I will forever". I said softly. She looked at me and smiled, "I love you too Simon and I will never stop". America its self held a large range of opportunities, after work each day I would go to the fights, it wasn't much just some low class men beating the crap out of each other, and who ever hit the mat first lost, it was a sport in America. I would spend half the day their drinking cheep liquor, and watching the fights, I remember that one day like any other I walked in and had some drinks, a couple of men, their names I wasn't sure asked if I was up to fight. I had had a long day and I was frustrated, so I said yes, the first round I lost to a large fat man with a mop of tangled black hair. I was bleeding from my mouth and my face unread, the next round was a stocky sort man, he was rather quick and hit with a ton of power, and I also lost to him. After the second round I stopped fighting and went home, rose was awake when I came through the door, and when she had a glimpse of my bloody face and beaten up fists she nearly gasped, "Simon, there will be no fighting in this house". She said hastily. I slowly took off my coat and ignored what she said, she ran towards me, "Simon did you hear me? I don't want you fighting". She said once more. I quickly turned towards her, "rose I know you don't want me to fight, but I have to". I said quickly. She rolled her eyes, "Simon, please sit down, so I can explain". I looked at her, "explain what, Hun I'm not killing anyone, so what is the problem"? I demanded. She was sitting by then her hands folded in her lap, "Simon, I'm worried about you, I've noticed that you have been drinking a lot and that you hardly come home at all, and when you do it's after hours when were asleep". She said in a sad tone.

I sighed, "ok rose, I do understand, but I'm not out killing, and this fighting takes my mind of wanting to kill". I said in a low voice. She smiled, "ok then fight, but don't become an alcoholic, I can't bear to see you like that". She said slowly and then went into the bedroom. I slowly sat down and rubbed my temples, my head was throbbing and my lip burned, I had to learn to fight, it was the only thing that took my mind away from wanting to kill. I went to the fights again that night but didn't fight I just watched, and learned the moves and the people who made them. 'You can learn a lot from watching a man fight'. And that's what I was doing there, I watched and learned, and before the nights end I would be a fighter. I went home after and immediately went to bed, rose was sound asleep, and the twins were sleeping also, but I slowly crept into their room and kissed each of their cheeks, and then tucked them in. I slept well that night, I dreamt of me fighting and wining like a champion, and then the dream faded off into me being in a funeral home, the casket was dark mahogany, topped with white roses, I woke before I could see the face off the dead inside. Rose was on top of me, and to no surprise she was nude, her body wasn't bad after having two babies, no real stretch marks, she was still thin and had the prettiest face I had ever seen. She slowly kissed my forehead we made love for the first time in months and it was amazing. She was already up before I awoke, trotted into the kitchen Edith was on the floor playing with some building blokes while edger was in the highchair playing with his food, I picked up Edith and kissed her cheek then tickled her until she stared to laugh to hard, rose took her into her arms and smiled at her, "daddy has to go to work big girl". By then Edgar was throwing his food all over the place and rose was at his side taking the food from his fingers. I went to work that day with a sense of accomplishment, how I don't know, but I felt great. I went to the fights after work as planned; I won the first round with a large African American, the second round I was up against a tall slender white man with a hell of a punch. The last round I lost to a large beefy man, he knocked me out and when I hit the mat I saw stars. I woke up in the hospital to my complete surprise, rose was at my side and the twins were on the ground playing with toys. She smiled when she saw me. "You got knocked out Simon, you had me so worried". She said in frustration. I smiled, "I'm ok sweet heart, just a headache". I said slowly. She rolled her eyes, "well the doors are running a few tests, and how in the entire world did I agree to marry your dumb ass"? She said bitterly. Looked up at her, "are you mad at me rose"? I asked in confusion. She sighed, "No I'm not mad at you, but you need to stop fighting Simon, you could get severely hurt or even die". She said her tone increasing. "Rose don't worry about me, I'm fine". I said pleading. She kissed me gently, and then a tall doctor came in, "afternoon Simon, so tell me what happed". He instructed. I sighed, "I just got knocked out that's all, why what's wrong with me"? I asked worried. He scratched his head and took a look at his papers, "says here that you suffer from random black outs, is that correct"? He asked in a professional tone. I nodded, "yeah sometimes, not lately though". I reported. He sighed, "Simon you have a brain tumor in the left side of your brain". He said slowly. I looked at rose who was all of a sudden in tears her face red and filled with worry. "Are you sure doctor"? I asked. He nodded, "yes, it's not a large tumor and it isn't growing but it is the reason for your black outs". He said slowly. "When am I going to die"? I asked quickly. Rose gasped and looked at me in horror, "Simon you're not going to die, so stop it". She scorned. I looked at her slowly, "rose everyone dies someday". I said bitterly she rolled her eyes and picked up Edith and kissed her on top of the head. The doctor was staring at me, "Simon no one knows how long you have, so I want you to come back next week so I can report on the changes". He informed. Rose looked at him, "doctor what can we do to stop the possible increase of it"? She asked in a low voice. He looked at me and sighed, "I suggest plenty of sleep and no more fighting". He said quickly then shook roses hand and left the room. Rose was already staring at me the second the doctor left, "you never told me you suffered from black outs". She said shortly. I looked at her and smiled, "I don't suffer from them, besides I haven't had any lately". I said quickly. She rolled her eyes, "it's the point Simon, and you could have prevented this if you would have told me earlier". She said in anger. "This is nothing to get worked up about rose". She looked at me and stood up, "what are you talking about, Simon you have a tumor in your brain, and that isn't something to be worried about"? She screamed. We left the hospital in silence, she was angry with me big time and I couldn't stand it, it was my body and if I had a tumor so what, not like there was anything anyone could do about it. I thought to myself. "Simon"? A voice screamed. But I was out of this world, "Simon"? It screamed again, I quickly looked around, rose was in my face, and "Simon are you ok"? She demanded. I smiled, "I'm fine, why"? I asked boldly. She huffed, "you will no longer fight Simon, its stupid and it's dangerous". She said loudly. I looked at her in frustration. "Rose fighting has nothing to do with this". I said calmly. She sighed,

"Simon yes it does, if you keep getting hit on your head then the tumor might grow or something, the point is Simon is that fighting is a stupid thing to do for fun". She said her face pouting a little. I sighed, "ok I won't fight anymore rose, I promise". I said while taking a deep breath. She smiled and kissed me. I never fought again, instead I started to gamble, at first all I did was win, but then my luck started to decline I stayed and gambled until I was broke and disappointed with myself for losing all the money I had earned. I would go home in frustration, rose would be sleeping and so would the twins, so I would just cuddle up to her and fall asleep. I stayed up most nights in pain and in sorrow, I was finally having a great life and when things were at their best I found out I had a brain tumor, I hated myself no doubt for all the horrid things I had done in my past, but never once did I think that they didn't disserve it. Besides I was only human sure I had my faults, but killing those people wasn't one of them, and if I miraculously had the option of going back and redo what I had done, I wouldn't have done it any different. I like killing no doubt and when I had their blood on my hands I felt invincible, it delivered me a sensation that I could never push away, I loved it the power of taking another's life with my own hands, I envied it and enjoyed it so. And I know took a vow with rose to never do it again but I yearned for it once more, I has a blood lust and I knew that nothing would ever be able to feed it but the blood of others. By now rose and I had lived in America for over two years, and the twins were growing up so well, rose and I hardly got in any fights since the finding out of my tumor, and it was sad to know that it took something tragic to stop it.

Chapter 7

known

As days turned to months and months into years rose and I gradually started to drift apart, I couldn't come home anymore without getting screamed at or being told what I was doing was incorrect. I'm not the greatest father I'll admit that much but I was trying, I tried to spend at least an hour a with the twins but mostly was only lucky if I got ten minutes in, rose was always on my case about the dumbest things, we could talk about something so mindless and then turn it into a fight. I hated coming home, so I started spending most of my time gambling and drinking, I wasted all my money and became a drunk in no time flat, and before the night end I was too drunk to even walk home and far too broke to call for a ride. Life had become nothing to me, my tumor was growing and there was nothing I or the doctors could do about it. I was falling apart at the seams, and it seemed that no matter how hard I tried to turn the tides, I would come out in the end the same or worse. Rose called me a 'ghost' all the time saying that I was never around to even be counted for, we hardly ever talked anymore, and to be honest I was scared to even try, knowing that it would only end in a fight of rage and hate. It wasn't long before rose decided it would be best for me to leave the house until I had all my ducks in a row, but my ducks had all died years ago, and I knew that she would never take me back even if I did have them straightened out. I rented a small apartment, but hardly spent any time in it. Rose permitted me to see Edger and Edith every week for a couple of hours, but it was never enough, and the moment they disappeared I felt a vast ocean of loneliness and self hatred. I remember the first night I killed again, it was cold outside, and I could clearly see my breath, my cheeks burned from the cruel night grief as I wandered the lonely streets, she was sleeping when I found her, she had ebony hair and ivory skin, she was a goddess I slowly walked up to her and sat beside her, she turned and looked at me, she had the face of an angle, two radiant hazel eyes stared up at me in curiosity, it was so east to lure her in, I slowly grazed her breast with my hand and caressed her face, she smiled at me and giggled, I drew her face close to mine and kissed her forcefully, she backed away and unbuttoned her dress, I watched as it fell to her feet, surrounding her ankles like a pool of water. She smiled and came closer to me, then gradually started to pull my pants down, I wanted her so badly, I then pulled her onto my lap and had my way, she moaned and screamed in pleasure, and after the last moan I pulled my knife out of my coat pocket and slashed her dainty throat, after I killed her I was drowning in my own laughter, it felt so good, and twenty times better than any sex could do. She screamed a little but not loud enough to alert anyone, I slowly wiped the knife off on her dress and then laid her flat o her back, I then carved two letters into her chest, S and L; for Simon lucre. I wanted people to know I was out there, I wanted them to know I had no mercy or guilt; I wanted them to be afraid, to be afraid of me. It was in the morning papers the very next day.

'A body of a young woman was found last night, she was murdered in cold blood, stripped of her clothing with two letters engraved into her chest S and L, if anyone has a clue of who could have performed these horrid actions or has any clue of what these letters mean please contact the police department.

As I read about this my heart actually skipped a beat, I was surprised how fast the media actually traveled in America. I went to see the twins that day but was pushed into the hall when I tried to get inside, "Simon you did it again didn't you"? She screamed. I smiled "rose I'm not here, for a fight with you, I came only to see the twins". I said slowly. She rolled her eyes, "whatever Simon, before I even let you in there, tell me the truth, did you kill that woman last night in the alley"? She asked in frustration. I smiled, "I don't think that's any of your business rose". I said coolly she smiled, "it was you, wasn't it you just can't stop, you're a monster Simon and you smell like booze". She lectured I sighed, rose can I see my children"? I asked frustrated. She gave me an angry look, "are you civilized enough to manage"? She asked sarcastically. "Just get out of my way rose, they are my kids too". I yelled. "They are mine too Simon, and don't you forget that". She said hastily then moved out of my way. The twins were three by then and they were so beautiful, Edith had short curly blonde hair with baby blue eyes, and Edgar had black hair with hazel eyes. I loved them so much, and it hurt me inside knowing that we would never be together. After an hour of spending quality time with the twins rose pulled me into the bedroom, she sat on the bed with her hands folded into her lap, she stared up at me, and "Simon I miss you, and so do the twins, and if you won't come back for me then come back for their sake". She cried. I sighed, "I'm not well rose I'll be honest, and frankly I don't trust myself around you or the twins, I think this is for the best". I said slowly. She sighed out loud and stood up, she slowly took my hands in hers, "you know what's funny"? She asked in deep thought. "What"? I asked quickly. "That even though you have put me through so much grief and hate, I can still say that I love you and that never once did I stop"?

She whispered not looking at me. I slowly drew her face to mine, "rose I never stopped loving you either, and I never will, but I'm sick rose I'm real sick this time, I can't stop it I try so hard, but it's not enough it's never enough". I cried. She looked at me sadly, "Simon if you keep doing caught eventually Simon, and you know that, you can't change the past but you can always create your own future" she said quickly. At that her hands dropped and she wiped her eyes, "Simon, please try to change, Simon just change for us for the kids please". She pleaded. I left rather quickly I wasn't in a hurry but I wanted to be, I had to get away I needed to clear my mind, my head was throbbing and I felt so sick, I knew what I needed, one thing something horrid to kill again. I walked the streets all day, yes I was tired and yes I was cold but I didn't care, I was drowning in my own self pity and I hated it, I hated myself far worse. I'm not certain of what time it was when I located my next victim, it was dark out and only the gas lamps lit the streets, I must have been walking for hours before I came across her, I stopped and hid behind a corner and watched her, a tall slender brown haired woman was walking out of a restraint, she wrapped her shawl around her shoulders and headed the opposite direction. I followed her, slowly moving as she did, taking steps as slowly as she did, I followed her into an alley; she stopped at a small door on the right side of a tall building. I quickly walked up behind her, "my lady, are you lost"? I asked in a pleasant way. She smiled and tightened her grip on her shawl. "No I'm fine, but thank you". She said slowly. "Well might I walk you home, it is cold out here and it isn't safe for a radiant beauty like yourself to be wandering off alone"? I assured. Her cheeks turned red and she smiled, "what a gentleman you are, that would be wonderful and possibly I might be able to repay you". She said smiling then slowly grazed her breast with her hand. I smiled, "I would like that miss". I said smiling. "I'm Claudia Mertzon, and you are"? She asked then smiled, "my name is William Luray It's nice to meet you Claudia". I said then kissed her hand gently. She laughed and pulled me close to her. "My house is down another couple of blocks". She giggled. I smiled, "well it's nice to meet a lady with so many manners". I quickly said. As we came into view of her house she stopped and smiled at me, "well aren't you coming in"? She begged. I smiled, "I suppose, who could deny you Claudia"? I asked. She laughed and pulled me inside then took me to her room and pushed me on the bed, "stay here stud, I'll be back". She ordered. I smiled and sat still, this was going way too far, I would quickly have sex with this beauty and when she couldn't go any further would slit her throat. She came in the room seconds later with a transparent silk nightgown. She slowly crawled on top of me and kissed me passionately, she undid my pants and filled the room with moans of delight and laughter, then in a blink of an eye I quickly slashed her throat with one quick movement, I then did the same laid her flat and carved my entitles, into her chest. Afterwards I went home and cleaned up, I slept well that night and woke later than usual. I went into town and bought another paper, and on the front paper was another article.

<u>'Another body of a young woman was found last night, she too was murdered in cold blood, stripped of her clothing with the same two letters engraved into her chest once again if anyone has a clue of who could have performed these horrid actions or has any clue of what these letters mean please contact the police department. We are now taking immediate action to locate the whereabouts of this killer; we are asking that all women and children stay indoors at night, to further prevent any more deaths.</u>

I loved it, oh it brought such overpowering joy to my heart, and they were 'taking immediate action'! Ha they would never find me I was too bright and way too careful. I went to see the twins that day, rose let me inside when I arrived and I spent an hour with the kids, afterwards as I was about to leave rose pulled me into the room, "Simon you've done it again haven't you"? She demanded bitterly. I smiled, "done what"? I asked sarcastically. "Simon these women you are killing are innocent people, they have families and possibly children, and how is it so damn easy to take another's life? She screamed while in tears. I pulled her head up, "rose what I have learned in my life so far is that it is far easier to take a life then to actually give one"? She quickly backed away from me, "you have issues Simon and you need help, I don't want you coming around here anymore, you're a sick bastard and I don't want my kids to be around that sort of thing". She said in anger. I smiled, "they are my kids also rose, or have you forgotten? Frankly I don't care what you say; if you try to stop me from seeing my kids rose I will end you so fast that even you won't see it coming". I threatened in a serious voice then left I went home after that and took a nap, I was so tired, I woke to a sudden knock on my door, I slowly opened it, and in front of my door stood a small child, she had blonde matted hair, and green eyes, I smiled, "what are you doing here little girl"? I asked kindly. She didn't say anything though she just stared at the floor and swayed back and forth. "Little girl, where are your parents"? I asked impatiently. She still didn't say anything, I quickly but softly placed my hands on her small shoulders, causing her to suddenly flinch, her eyes moved up to mine and on her left cheek was the bruise of a handprint. I quickly stepped back, "hey little girl who did that to your lovely face"? I asked half hoping she would actually answer. She just wiped her eyes and didn't speak, "what's your name little girl? I'm sure you have one so tell me". I said in frustration. She sniffled, "my name is Ava, and I don't know where my mommy is" she cried tears falling to the floor in large drops I smiled, "well where did you see her last"? I questioned. She then started to cry louder, "I don't know, I want my mommy". She cried. "What happened to your face Ava"? I asked again. She looked up at me and wiped her eyes, "mommy told me not to tell". She said in a whisper. "Well I'm your friend so you can tell me, I promise to not tell anyone". I said slowly. She sniffled a little and then scratched her head, "you promise with your heart"? She asked seriously. I nodded, "with all of it". I said. She slowly fiddled her fingers and rubbed her nose.

"It was an accident, she didn't mean to". She cried suddenly. I sighed, "Well where, is your mommy now, I want to talk to her". I said in anger. She quickly looked at me with wide eyes, then turned around, and walking towards us was a short fat woman, "Ava what are you doing over there, get your ass over here right now". She screamed. I quickly looked at Ava, "do you want to go with her"? I asked quickly she shook her head immediately, "Ava I said right now, if you don't get over hear I'll whoop your little ass until it bleeds". She screamed. I looked at Ava, "I want you to go sit on the couch and close your eyes and cover your ears, and can you do that for me Ava"? I asked. She nodded and went and sat down, I slowly shut my door and went into the hall, and the woman looked at me confused, "what are you doing, where is my daughter"? She screamed coming towards me. "Did you hurt that little girl"? I asked. She smiled, "what business is it of yours"? She screamed. I smiled, "do you like to hurt your daughter"? I asked coming towards her, by then she was swimming in a lake of fear she started to back away, "what do you want"? She asked in desperation. I smiled, "do you want to see what I feels like to be hurt all the time"? I asked. She backed away quickly, "don't you come any further or ill call the cops" she threatened. I smiled, "then do it, call them I'm sure they would love to see what you've been doing to that little girl". I screamed. She kept backing up and I just kept coming forward "so call them, what are you waiting for"? I asked. She quickly looked around her, "what are you going to do"? She asked in a worried tone. I sighed, "how about I kill you or how about I just beat the living crap out of you?" I asked. She immediately went down to her knees and started to cry, "Oh please don't hurt me". She begged. I slowly inched closer to her, but stopped at arm's length. "If you ever hurt that girl again, while you are sleeping I will come into your room and slit you throat, is that clear you old miserable hag"? I threatened my tone increasing. She quickly started to nod her head, "yes, yes, and yes". She repeated. I slowly went into my house and kneeled down in front of Ava, "your mother won't ever hurt you again, but Ava if she does I want you to come here and knock on my door as many times as it takes and if I don't answer just keep knocking". I instructed. She nodded and quickly jumped into my arms and squeezed me tight, "ok Ava you can go now, but remember what I told you". She smiled and nodded then left. I felt like a hero for a split second after Ava left, she was so cute but her mother was an abusive wench. I left the apartment after that and by then it was getting dark out, the moon was high above though and the stars twinkled in the cold, once again I prowled the streets in search of that perfect victim, I knew that many people would stay indoors at night after the news paper, but I didn't care it was America people did what they wanted when they wanted, I slowly walked the alleys only to find no one lingering in them so I went to the other side of the housing departments, I watched from the corner of a building, two men were pushing around a woman, she was pleading for them to stop but they just laughed and continued, so I approached them, the men were drunk and the girl was a prostitute, they were fighting about whether or not the woman had slept with the taller man for free, "is there a problem here madam"? I asked kindly but was answered by the taller man, "Are you looking to get killed man"? He asked in a vicious tone. I smiled, "no but I think I was talking to the lady". I said quickly. He looked at the other man and laughed, "This bastard wants to die". He chuckled. I quickly lifted the woman off the ground, her face was bloody and she was hardly able to stand, I wrapped her arms around my shoulders and started to take her away, but was pulled back by my coat by the taller man, he yanked me back causing the woman to fall to the ground again, "kid I think it would be best for you to just go back to where you came from, and leave the woman we can handle it". He chuckled. I quickly shoved him back, "I'm leaving now and I'm taking her with me". I said angrily. The men both looked at each other and broke out in laughter, "man if ya want a whore that bad I would prefer one that is more alive, unless your into that sort of thing". He laughed. I knew I was out numbered and right now I was like a mouse up against two cobras, it was a no win situation I would lose and I knew it, but I would try. I quickly picked her up again and leaned her over me, then again the man pulled me back causing her to once again fall. I quickly jumped up and punched him in the jaw, he slowly lost his balance, blood was pouring out of his nose he smiled at me and came forward I was hit then and I saw stars, but I got back up. I tried once more to take the girl, but was knocked to the ground then kicked several times in the face, then like before the voices blurred and all went white I had been knocked out. I imagined I would wake in the hospital but this time I woke up in the spot where I was knocked out, my head was spinning and I felt I'll as I slowly stood up I noticed that the woman I had tried to save was staring at me from the to of a porch, her face wasn't bloody any longer but now entirely black and blue. She smiled at me, "who are you anyway"? She asked quickly. I looked up at her, "my name is Simon, and you are"? I asked. She sighed, "my name is Mora'. She replied. I smiled, "that's a lovely name". She smiled and blushed. "What were you doing out here last night"? She asked. "I might ask you the same question". I replied. She smiled, "I live here, and those men well the taller one is my boss and the other was a client". She said slowly. "How old are you Mora"? I asked quickly. She looked at the ground, "I'll be 18 next month". She said briefly. "Now tell me what you were doing"? She asked. I smiled, "I was only out for a walk when I saw those men beating on you". I replied while looking at the ground. She laughed, "You were taking a walk? Why would you take a walk in the most dangerous part of America"? She asked surprised. Smiled, "well it brought me to you". I said slowly. She sighed and rubbed her cheek, "well do you want to do some business"? She asked in a provocative way. I smiled, "I can't; besides you should rest". I said slowly. She quickly grabbed my wrist, "please it's the most I can do for your help last night". She said quickly. "There is no need for anything; I helped you only because what they were doing was wrong". I said kindly and started to leave. "Please let me help you Simon". I turned to look at her only to find her stark naked, I smiled faintly, "look Mora what your trying to do is great and highly respected but I have to go now, I'm surly great full possibly another time". I muttered then went back to my dwelling

Chapter 8

the case

It was high noon when I got there and I was exhausted my cheek burned from the fight and I was way too tired to even eat anything, so instead I just went to sleep. I woke to a loud banging noise and then a faint scream, I quickly jumped up and went next door, I pounded on the door for several minutes, nothing but crying and screams answered me back. I was panicking at the moment if I didn't get in their she would kill that little girl, and for a second I wondered why I was so nervous about the situation, after another high pitched scream I broke the door down, the mother was standing at the foot of a small bed with a gun in her hand pointed at Ava, she looked at me then to her mother, then let out another shriek, the mother turned towards me and laughed, "it's too late boy, she is already dead at that she pulled the trigger which ended in a loud painful cry, I quickly pushed the mother to the ground and picked the gun up and moved it, then ran over to Ava, she was lying it what seemed to be a ocean of blood, it was gushing out of her chest and when I tried to stop it, it only came out in large quantities I quickly picked her up and kissed her head, "Simon I'm sorry". She whispered then fell wilted in my arms, tears were swarming down my face by then and I felt so hot I ran her to the hospital, knowing she had already died. Two doctors put her on a stretcher and hauled her away, that's when I noticed I was drenched in blood so I ran home and changed and burned the clothes and then went back to the hospital, and the moment I stepped in my lags caved in when she was taken and I stopped breathing, I suddenly became very cold and I finally fainted. I woke to rose's face in mine she was crying and holding my hand tight, "hi baby". I said faintly. She then started crying harder, "where is the girl, the little girl where is she"? I screamed. Then at the snap of a finger a doctor came in and a police man in his steps the male doctor came forth first, "where is the little girl"? I cried he shook his head in disappointment, "she's gone Simon". He said boldly. I sat up quickly, "no it's not true, she is alive please doctor tell me she's alive". I pleaded. He just shook his head, "Simon she's gone, the wound was too great". He said slowly. I again collapsed in tears, "Simon how did you come by his accident'? A fat officer asked in a skeptic tone. I looked at him disgusted, "her and her mother live next to me, I woke to screams and loud smacking sounds, I'm not sure what was going in their officer, so I was quite disturbed to hear that noise, I went and knocked on the door several times but I never had an answer, just more screams. So I knocked down the door, and that woman was holding a gun and it was pointed at the little girl Ava". I while I was spilling my guts about this poor child. I was in a deep thought, about who was to be my next victim, and that's when I remembered that girl Mora, she was perfect for my plan her blood would nourish the earth, but it could also nourish me I could drink it . . . couldn't I?" The officer looked at me, "well what happened after that?" I smiled quickly only to please this total moron, he was a lowlife scum bag and death awaited him very quickly. "Ok so Ava was standing on the bed, and her mother was standing at the edge of the bed, she then pulled the trigger and shot her. I tried to stop her, but if I came any closer she threatened to shot her. Officer that woman killed that little girl". His head was bent down and he was sobbing inside. "Why am I a suspect?" I quickly asked aloud. He smiled and tipped his hat, "well be in touch". He said then walked away. I was so scared by then, I did nothing wrong I tried to save her life and I failed and I felt horrible, but to consider me a suspect was way out of line. I quickly looked at rose; she shook her head in frustration, then gathered up the twins and left me there. I wasn't allowed to leave the hospital, so when I was better I was immediately escorted to the jail and spent the night in a small cinderblock cell, and the minute I woke up I was again escorted, but to the interrogation room, I walked in and was immediately bored to death, the room was awfully bland and white paint enclosed the room, in the middle was a small wooden table and upon it was a bottle of water and a tape recorder, I slowly sat down on the plastic chair and folded my hands in my lap, a short fat man walked in and gave me a serious scowl, "detective Williams will be here in a few seconds". He reported then left with a hurry. As the name escaped his fat mouth I nearly choked on my own tongue, it was him, that detective from London, he followed me here and now he was going to end me and all that I had worked for. I was trembling with fear, and my body was completely numb. It wasn't long before he walked in, he looked the same, his blonde hair was a little longer and upon his round head was a bowler hat, a black satin ribbon complimenting it. He smiled as he walked in, a clip board in his hands. "It's nice to see you again Simon, and how have you been"? He asked in sarcasm. I sighed and stared at the floor, he slowly walked towards me, I quickly looked at him, and "I didn't kill that girl Williams". I screamed. He shrugged his shoulders, "I never said you did, but if you didn't kill her then why were your fingerprints on the gun and why did you change your clothes"? He asked a sly smile playing across his face. I looked at him shocked, "well Simon, can you tell me why"? He asked as he sat down across from me. "I want a lawyer". I said boldly. He nodded his head and smiled, "why, are you nervous?" he asked shyly. I smiled, "why do I look tense?" I asked mockingly. He smiled, "the minute I saw you Simon, I instantly liked you". He said in a booming laugh. I smiled, "well I'll have you know I never liked you". I said bitterly. He sighed, "Well you had better start because I think you and I will start seeing each other a lot more". He said quickly. I smiled, "and why is that"? I asked. He sighed, "Well because Simon you're a suspect, like I said your prints were all over that gun, the same gun that took the life of Ava Roland". He said all this in a half professional way. I looked at him, "when I left the apartment her mother was still there she didn't care at all, so I brought her to the hospital, is that a crime? I tried to save her". I confessed. He sighed, "Well the report says that there was one shot fired, at eleven thirty". He said slowly. I cradled my head in my hands for several minutes, "I didn't kill her, and I would never harm that girl". I said clearly. He cleared his throat and looked at me, "so if you didn't kill her then why in the hell, were your prints on the gun"? "And also if you didn't kill her then why did you change your clothes"? He asked in frustration. I looked up at him, "I want a lawyer". I said firmly. He sighed, "I understand that Simon". He replied. "No I don't think you do". I replied in anger. He smiled, "you're charged with homicide Simon, if you're fortunate you'll get five to ten years and that's all". He said standing up. "Simon if you didn't kill that girl then why on all earth did you pick up that gun"? He asked walking towards the door. "I'm not going to discuss this with you or anyone until I have a lawyer". I said lastly. He nodded and left.

I was then escorted back to the same cell, I didn't sleep that night I was too heated, instead of being charged with the real killing I preformed I was being charged with the murder of a little girl I didn't kill. The next day I was permitted a, phone call, who I was going to call I had no idea, so I called rose. She didn't say much and it seemed that she really didn't want to talk to me; I told her that she needed to immediately find a lawyer that could represent me and fast. She said ok then hung up. It was about a week before I actually met my lawyer, he was a tall lean man with a mop of neatly trimmed red hair, he looked like he was in his late twenties early thirties in his hand was a brown worn out brief case. I was brought to the interrogation room my lawyer following. The moment we stepped into the room he had his hand out for me to shake, "my name is Jude Haran; I will be representing you and your case". He said with a smile. I nodded, "I'm Simon lucre". I said slowly. He sighed, "So Simon what is going on"? He asked in a far too grave tone. "I'm being charged with, homicide". I said slowly. He nodded, then opened his brief case and took out a manila folder with my name in fine print written on top. He flipped through a few pages then stopped and looked up at me, "says here you shot Ava Roland". He said then quickly looked up at me. I shook my head, "I didn't kill her". He leaned back in the chair and smiled, "your prints were on the gun Simon, so if you didn't kill her then how on earth did they get their"? He asked in frustration. I ignored his question and bent my head down. "Look Simon if you want to win this case, then you're going to have to trust me and tell me the truth and nothing but the truth". He said quickly. I quickly looked up at him, "why does it matter you don't believe me"? I asked slowly. He let out a chuckle, "Simon I'm your lawyer I don't have to believe you and frankly I don't care, the only thing that matters is that you and I win this case". He muttered. "I didn't kill her". I mumbled. "Ok so you didn't kill her, but Simon you have to understand that your prints were all over that gun". I quickly stood up, "look I might have picked up that gun but I didn't kill them". I said as I walked around the table. He leaned back in the chair and wrote a note on the corner of a paper. "Why would you pick the gun up Simon if you didn't kill her"? He asked in a loud voice. I scratched my head and sat back down, "I don't know, she killed the girl, so I took the gun, it was a reaction". I said coolly. He smiled, "so let me get this straight, this girl Ava gets shot and out of reaction you pick up the gun, the same gun that killed her, is that correct"? He asked. I smiled, "look, think what you want, but I didn't murder her". I quickly screamed. He sat back and folded his hands on the table, "I never said you did Simon, I'm just curious of what was going through your head when that little girl died, and why on earth you picked up the gun". He laughed then pulled out a pack of cigarettes, and lit one up, "want one"? He asked pushing the pack towards me. I sighed and had one. "So

Simon you didn't kill her but you did pick up the gun". He asked in a mono tone. I nodded, "if I killed her then why did I waste my time bringing her to the hospital, can you answer that"? I said resentfully. He smiled and took another drag of his cigarette, "maybe when you shot her, you felt some anguish or possibly some distress, and brought her in". He said. I smiled, "I tried to save her life, it seems like everyone here is acting like that is a crime". I yelled. He smiled, "ok so you brought her in then why did you change your clothes"? He asked quickly, as he was looking down at the papers. I looked up at him, "I was covered in blood". I said slowly. He nodded, "where are the clothes Simon"? He asked. "I burned them". I muttered. He smiled and laughed, "Simon why would you burn the clothes"? He asked in a laugh. I looked up at him, "I don know why I burned them, I changed because I was covered in blood". I said quickly with a straight face. He laughed again, "So after you brought her to the hospital, you want home changed your clothes and burned the others"? I nodded, "I know how it sounds but you have to believe me". I pleaded. He sighed, "No Simon, I don't have to believe you, I just have to defend you". I cradled my head in my hands and closed my eyes, "where's my wife and kids"? I asked in anger. "At home I would imagine, Simon this has nothing to do with them, now tell me why you burned the clothes". He demanded. "I don't fucking know". I screamed. He quickly sat back, "well you had better start to know Simon, do you have any idea of what this looks like". He asked in anger his voice gradually increasing. I didn't answer I just closed my eyes. "Simon you're wanted for murder your prints are, on the murder weapon, and then you go and change your garments and burn the others, sounds to me like you did it, and if that's not enough have a great time trying to persuade a jury, knowing that they probably have children also". He said while standing up. I quickly looked up at him, "where are you going"? I asked quickly. He sighed, "were done for today, sleep on it Simon and when I come tomorrow have an idea of why you did what you did". At that he left. I then was again brought to my cell; I just sat their lost in deep thought, 'why did I burn the clothes? Why did I pick up the gun?' I asked myself these questions all night.

As planned my lawyer came by at around noon, and like before we went into the interrogation room and sat down. "So Simon did you think about everything last night"? He asked firstly. I nodded, "yeah all night". He nodded and smiled, "great and what is your answer"? He asked impatiently. I sighed, "I burned my clothes because I was in shock and I didn't want any one too-". I paused and looked at him, and upon his face was distaste. "You didn't want to what?" he asked quickly. I sighed, "I didn't want anyone to think I did it". I mumbled. Shock danced across his face, "you didn't want anyone to think you did it"? He asked in anger "that is such horse shit Simon, why would you even think that if you already knew you didn't"? He demanded. I wiped my mouth and leaned back in the chair. "I was scared ok, I was covered in blood, what would you have done"? I screamed. He quickly took out a cigarette and quickly lit it, "it doesn't matter what I would have done, this case isn't about me, I'm not the one on death row Simon you are". He said in a nasty tone. "I know that, I would just like to know what you would have done". I said quickly. He sighed, "well I'll tell you this much, I definitely wouldn't of picked up the gun and I also wouldn't of burned my damn clothes". He said as he took another drag. He then quickly took out a piece of paper from is brief case, "says here that the mother of Ava is testifying against you, she claims that you broke into her home and pulled out a gun and shot her daughter". He replied. I looked at him in total disbelief, "she's lying, and that's not true". I screamed in rage. "No Simon I think your lying, why did you move to America"? He asked quickly. I looked at him, "I don't know". "Why does that matter"? I demanded. He gave me an evil look, "while you lived in London, a detective came to you didn't he? He was disturbed about the unexpected decease of your land lady Anita Ancline". He reported out loud. I nodded, "yes it was detective Williams, and he wanted to ask me some questions". "Did he ever ask those questions"? He asked. "No he didn't". I said shortly. "Why"? He asked. "I'm not sure". He looked at me and punched the table, "you liar Simon, you left, you suddenly vanished Simon, what were you hiding, what made you up and leave so quickly"? He demanded in frustration. I smiled, "I don't know, why don't you tell me"? I said in a sarcastic tone. "Because you killed her Simon, why else would you up and disappear when a detective came around looking for answers, its so plain Simon". He screamed. I smiled again, "well bravo, I knew you were smart but that's another story, besides why are we talking about this, shouldn't we be discussing what we are going to do about this case"? I asked in sarcasm. He bent his head down and let out a deep breath, "you killed that little girl, didn't you"? He asked. I sighed, "No I didn't". I said quickly. He then jumped in my face, "you sick little fuck, just stop it Simon, your prints are on the gun you changed your clothes and burned the evidence, this game your playing isn't helping you Simon". He screamed his face turning a deep shade of red. I was in rage by then, "now you listen to me, you're my lawyer you do whatever the fuck I tell you when I tell you, I didn't kill that girl, yes I love blood, the sight of it makes me get off, but I didn't kill her". I said calmly. He looked at me in shock, "I'm getting you a psychological evaluation, before I waste anymore of my time with you". He said then stood up and headed for the door. "Where the fuck are you going"? I screamed. He turned back towards me, "you have no control over me you little bastard, I'll see you in a few days, bye Simon". He said then slipped out the door. I was in rage when he left, he was a pile of shit and I was out of luck with him representing me, I then was again brought back to my cell, I just sat on the bunk, I was given another phone call so I called rose, but not to talk to her but to talk to the twins. "Hi Simon, what do you want"? She asked in a skeptic tone. "I want to talk to the twins rose". I spewed. "Hi daddy I love you, when are you coming home"? Edith asked in her small voice. I didn't answer for a couple of minutes I was so screwed, "I'll be home in a few days and can I talk to your brother"? I asked slowly. "Hi dad, I miss you, I learned how to tie my shoes dad". He cried in happiness. I smiled at that as tears rolled down my cheeks. "I love you dad, mom wants to talk to you". He said rose's voice crackled over the phone, "Simon what is going on with the case? Did you kill that girl? Should I even ask you that?" she questioned. "Rose I didn't do it and the case is going fine". I said lastly. I listened as a deep sigh came over the phone, "I have to go Simon". She quickly said. "Rose I love you". I said quickly. But by then she had already hung up. My lawyer didn't come for another three days, and when he did it was the same routine. "So Simon how have you been"? He asked as he sat down across from me. "Like shit and you"? I asked not caring the least bit. "Next week is your first hearing Simon, and we hardly have a case, so I'm dedicating today to make one". He said as he lit a cigarette. I looked up at him, "well why don't you have one yet"? I asked. He looked at me skeptically, "because it's hard to make one when my client isn't helping". He said flushed. I smiled, "and I'm not helping how"? I asked. He quickly stood up and paced around the room, "Simon you still haven't told me why you picked the gun up or why you burned your clothes". He muttered as he circled the table. "ok I burned my clothes because I was scared and I picked the gun up because I was afraid she, the mother would kill me or herself". I reported slowly and clearly. By then he was jotting all that I was saying down on a manila note pad. He set the pen down and looked up at me, "why were you scared"? He asked suddenly. I sighed, "I was covered in blood, there was a dead girl, and I panicked". I sputtered. A large smiled played on his lips, "so you panicked and that made you burn your blood saturated clothes"? He asked looking at his note pad. I nodded, "yes that's' why I burned them". I said in a low voice. He smiled, "so Simon when we go into the hearing, you keep your mouth shut, I say everything not you". I smiled and quickly nodded, "I understand but shouldn't I tell what happened"? I asked. He looked up at me, "did you pay attention to what I said, you say nothing, and keep your mouth shut and we will be fine". He yelled in frustration. I arched my back and popped my knuckles, "so am I guilty or not guilty"? I asked in an innocent voice. "Do I get bail"? He looked at me, "bail may be set at the discretion of the judge, then you will be notified when and where to attend next, if bail is denied you will be remanded into custody". He replied in a monotone. I put my head down and closed my eyes, "and after that"? I asked quickly. He cleared his voice and sighed, "Well after that you will go to a preliminary hearing, I'm sure this case will reach state level so seven to ten days after the last hearing you will go before a district justice, they then will determine if the case merits will go any further". "Now the prosecution has to prove by a prima facie case that the charges are valid, then they will call witness if any and they will show the evidence. I doubt that the case will go to federal court so it will immediately go to grand jury, there are 32 citizens, and you may leave the courtroom to confer with me when you feel the need. Unlike actual trials, guilt may be inferred by you exercising your right not to testify. Within the next 30 days, the formal arraignment takes place. The filing of Information's, which is a list of those charges accepted in the preliminary trial, is recorded. You may then plead for each charge. Typically, you plead not guilty, or stand mute. After 30 more days pass, the pre-trial conference is held, this leads to the guilt phase, assume you decide not to plead guilty, during the formal arrangement. If you do plead guilty you are admitting to factual guilt. Now say you decide to plea nolo that means you will accept any sentence handed down to you, but you don't admit factual guilt, so basically you can get off sooner with a lesser sentence, now you can also do a Alford plea which means you plead guilty but asserting actual innocence, you then would plead accountable but to a lesser charge to avoid a death sentence". He informed in his usual professional tone. I looked at him awkwardly, "so which would I plead"? I asked frustrated with all the options. He smiled, "depends if your guilty or not". He smirked. "Well I want an Alford plea". I said sternly. He smiled, "frankly it's not up to you to decide". He replied hastily. "Now if you do plead not guilty we will immediately go to jury selection, at the next step, the judge will give opening instructions to the jury Next, the opening statements are heard After the judge will then give closing instructions to the jury on how to proceed. The jury will come back with a verdict once a unanimous 12 to 0 decision is reached. The judge will poll the jury, to verify each juror has come to the same decision. If the verdict is not guilty, you are free to go. If you are found accountable, you will be sentenced to serve time, and will be remanded into custody." I looked at him eagerly, "am I going to get time"? I asked quickly. He sighed, "I have no idea, and it's not up to me it's completely up to the jury". He replied in deep thought. "Do you think I have a chance"? I asked quickly. He shrugged his shoulders and sighed, "I don't know Simon". I sighed, "Do you think I will, honestly?" I asked again. He sighed, "Possibly, they do have a witness and the weapon, and so at any time they can bring it forth". It seemed as if the day never ended, as if it lingered on simply repeating itself over and over again, when in this oh so famous cell, I didn't sleep or even really think, my mind was a vast ocean of darkness, I just sat in the corner of the cell, by then I wore different clothes, my usual black pants were now a pair of dark gray sweats, and my button up shirt was a short sleeve teal flannel shirt. I had no shoes or socks just bared feet, which were black from the build up of dirt and scum. My russet hair wasn't brown any longer but now a black, saturated in grease and grime, and entirely tousled, my teeth had a build up of muck and residue from the boiler and they were slowly decomposing, but I was decaying far faster, my body ached and my limbs shook, you can consider me spineless or even self-regarding. I was shrinking and my legs were cramped and if I dared to stand I would cave in, the air around me was retched and frigid, chilling my very bones and the place had persistence attar of decaying wood and food, accompanied by the desolate stench of rotting flesh. My mind was eating away at my body; I was dying from the inside out, and in the vast emptiness of the universe I was like a speck of dirt on someone's shoe, no one cared I didn't even care anymore, how could I? Seriously I was like an animal in a cage, randomly getting poked at, I hated the world, and America far more, I moved here to get away from my troubles, and now I was being locked into a cell for something I didn't do, it wasn't fair none of it was, I just didn't get the concept of my cruel and unfair handling, the food wasn't much at the prison, usually some multi colored slop thrown into a bowl given to us with a plastic spoon, it tasted foul also as you can guess, like a mix between old musty vegetables and vomit. I hardly ate it, I became extremely slender, and I refused to devour it. As days became weeks and weeks into months, before long I had been locked up for three years, my lawyer hadn't had a great deal of luck with getting me off, so when the decision came into play and the jury decided, I was found guilty of first degree murder and I was to serve six years in prison, and it wasn't before long before I invited death, I loathed being locked up, and in death I would be ultimately liberated. No one ever stopped by to see me in the first three years I was in, and I hadn't seen the twins in ever and I knew that by now that they would probably be three or four. She wore a yellow dress when she entered the waiting room, fuchsia flowers printed across it, her golden hair was tied up and a few pieces dangled at her shoulders, she looked stressed when she came in a vexed look displayed across her face, bur even if she looked distressed her eyes still sparkled and her skin glowed. She never once looked into my eyes, and when I tried to touch her hand she jerked away, she hardly spoke and when she finally did it was awful news, she didn't smile or frown, just a straight face, "Simon were leaving America, the twins and I are going back to London. We have waited for you as long as we can, I'm sorry Simon but you're lost to us, America it chaotic now, the streets are compacted with rivalries and I'm afraid to even leave the house". Their wasn't anything that I could even say while she was mumbling, but I did get a shiver up my spine, she was finally leaving and their wasn't anything that I could even do about it, I looked up at her and her face by then was relaxed, "Rose please don't leave, I don't have much time left, just wait please just wait a little longer". I begged on the verge of tears. She was on her feet by then, "Simon I can't and I won't, I'm sorry Simon but we have to move on, so I guess this is goodbye". She said lastly then started for the door, but as she was turning I caught her wrist and pulled her close to me, "I'm sorry rose for what I've done and how badly I've torn us apart". I quickly said then let her go. Her eyes widened and she started to cry, she quickly pulled my face to hers and she kissed me for the last time. As she walked to the door she turned around and smiled, "Simon we will wait for you, as long as it takes, just come home when you get out". She said lastly then left.

Chapter 9

damned in prison

While I was being escorted back to the cell, I made a plan in my head, that when I got out I would find rose and my children; I would make her forgive me, I would make her take me back. But a fraction of my mind doubted it highly, I would never get out I would remain a locked up animal for all of time. During the last three years in prison I longed for the blood of others, I needed to kill. By the end of the night I was in a fit of chills, and the smell of the place made me nauseous and literally sick to my stomach. I didn't have a cell mate for the first three years, and then one day I was given one, his name was Samuel, he was skinny and quite petite he had blonde sandy hair that fell at his ears with two shit brown eyes, he was on death row for the murder of his wife and her secrete lover, supposedly he walked in on them in bed went out to the shed, grabbed an axe, went inside and slaughtered them both in a fit of rage. He didn't seem ashamed, and he claimed he was innocent but then again *everyone in prison is innocent*. He didn't talk much, and for a while I thought he was retarded or something. I let him have the bottom bunk and I took the top, he wasn't a large man by any means, he was stocky and quite muscular but short, very short. By then I was on my fourth year in prison, and he on his first but I knew he wasn't getting out; well then again he would be but in death. Time seemed to go by slower than ever, and I was loosing my mind, I had two years left in this crummy place, and it seemed as if time itself had completely stopped, in prison I earned the reputation of the devil on the block, how I've not a clue. In prison no one called anyone by their first name, just some gang names or some low life slang. But in the beginning I was pushed around frequently and was ordered to do everything for my fellow inmates, to be frank I was everyone's bitch, they pushed me around and made jokes about me, but I changed that one special day, it was the normal morning I was sprawled across my bunk, staring up at the ceiling when a tall negro walked in by the name of Calvin, he grabbed me by my ankles and swung me off my bunk causing me to hit my head on the toilet seat which was in the corner, blood poured from a large gash above my eyebrow and I nearly fainted, but I gained conchesness and then jumped back up and pushed him back. But it didn't faze him, he just kept coming foreword. He was bigger then me and definitely stronger too, in prison he was that guy that you don't fuck with, an insane guy who would kill you for even looking his way. He then came forward with great speed and swung at my face in rage, but I flinched back and ducked under him, in the wall behind my pillow was a shank made of thick plastic sharpened to a point I had made the first year I came, I knew already that I wouldn't have enough time to retrieve it, so I immediately had to think of a way to get him far enough back to retrieve it. but just as he was about to deck me Samuel walked in a drew his fist, I saw a twinkle in his eye and for a split second a shit eating grin danced across his face, and he grabbed Calvin's wrist and snapped it, so I quickly retrieved the shank and stuck it through his neck. I watched as blood poured out from the pin size hole, and then it happened, my body went numb and lapsed into a fit of spasms, it was an overpowering feeling and I nearly crumbled to the ground. Samuel was standing over Calvin in the door way, with an anxious face. "Simon what are we going to do about this"? He asked pointing down at Calvin who was now completely dead; two eyes stared up at me, black and glossed over. "I don't know". I sputtered quickly. He smiled, "don't worry man; I'll take the blame, besides I'm dying in the end anyways". He laughed.

It wasn't long before a herd of security guards came to our cell; they shoved us up against the wall and thoroughly patted us both down. The warden was a short fat man, and frankly I'm not surprised he walked in and looked at us both, "who did this?" he asked sharply. I was about to confess but Samuel punched me in the stomach, causing me to lose my breath, "I did it, that bad ass punk deserved it". He said quickly glancing at me with a grin. The warden then took a handkerchief from his pocket and coughed into it then waved the security guards in to take him away. He then was taken to the box; the box is a small closet like shack which lies underground, dark and unbearable. As they hauled him away I went and laid down on my bunk, I was about to close my eyes when a voice made me open them, "I know you did it, I saw you" It said. I quickly jumped up and looked around, in the door stood a little old man; he had long brown hair which hung at clumps at his mid back, "well what do you want"?

I asked quickly now frustrated. He just smiled a toothy grin. "Nothing at all, what's your name son"? He asked. "Simon". I replied in a hastily tone. "And you are"? I asked rather quickly. He sighed, "On the block I'm called goblin, but my real name is Harold". He said smiling. I nodded, "why are you called that"? I asked in curiosity. Goblin shrugged his shoulders, "I'm not really sure, I think it's my height". He replied. I smiled and sat back down, so what is it you want"? I asked slowly. He smiled, "do you mind"? He asked pointing at the lower bunk. "No go ahead". I replied. He slowly sat down, "Calvin was a nasty man, probably the most feared on our entire block". "You're point"? I asked. "People are going to look at you differently now Simon". I looked at him quickly, "why would they do that, no one knows about this but you and me". I assured. He shook his head instantly, "things spread like diseases in prison, and everyone knows you killed Calvin". He informed. By then my head was in my hands, "so what happens now"? I asked in worry. He quickly patted my shoulder, "don't worry man; I will be your personal look out man". He informed. I gave him a just look, "dude your like sixty, how are you going to do that"? I asked in a doubtful tone. "I may be old but I've been in here long enough to know my shit, I have respect in here, and I suggest you start to respect me also". He said while standing up. "Ok, ok help me, what do I do"? I asked in desperation. He smiled, "nothing unusual, just act like you, but you don't have to take anyone's shit anymore, you've earned our respect Simon, hmmm .... Simon, that name has to change, for now on your called devil". He said lastly then left me. Devil, I thought in my head, it wasn't normal but then again nothing is in prison. Meal time was a different story that day, usually I sat by myself or with Samuel, but today I was called to several different tables, their were several gangs in prison you had you skins, your bloods your crypts your colored your Asian and your spicks. But that day I sat next to goblin and a few other men, he smiled and waved me over, before I was about to sit he stood up and cleared his voice, all eyes moved to him, "listen up you little shits, this man here is devil and you had better respect him". He said pointing at me. Heads nodded and whisperers filled the room. He quickly pulled me down by him, "eat devil, you're going to need your strength in the yard today". He instructed. I looked at him, "why is that"? I asked quickly. He smiled, "because you're going to have to fight". He replied and took another bite of his slop, I looked at him warily, "fight? Why would I have to fight?" I asked. He looked at me skeptically, "right now you're at the top of the list and the men in here want your spot so, in the yard you're going to have to fight, if you die then the man who did it takes your spot and it begins all over again". He replied smugly. "That's crazy, so I'm wanted dead now?" I asked hoping he would say no. he smiled, "yes from here on out you're the top priority, everyone and everyone's cousin wants you dead now, so stay close to me and don't die". He said then took another bite. He patted my back, "eat devil, we can't have you fighting on an empty stomach". He chuckled. I ate as slow as I could but I still had to go to the yard, once I stepped onto the cement I was ran at my a tall negro, he swung fast and hard and hit me in the left temple, I wasn't fast enough so I saw stars, he them came at me again, goblin was staring at me with wide eyes, "get em devil". He screamed. And not before long a circle of inmates were inclosing us. I came at him fast and with a great deal of force knocked him on his ass, blood seeped out of his nose, and he was curled into a ball, cheers erupted out of the crowd, and for a split second bliss filled my veins. And not before long another inmate came at me, a skin to be precise, he swung at my face, but I dodged it, causing him to loose his balance and go forward. After the days end and night fell upon the prison, I was in a mass amount of pain, my head spun all night and I broke my nose. I didn't sleep and right, but when I started to drift off I heard a loud thud from the cell next to mine accompanied by a scream and loud yelling. Seconds later I heard a few moans and some intense cries then the noise stopped all together. The morning started abruptly, the warren decided to have a surprise cell check, so the security guards came around and trashed our cells, usually never finding anything. And when they were at my cell I nearly choked because I knew they would find my shank which was still behind the cinderblock in the wall. They didn't find it but they did trash my cell, so I spent the morning cleaning it up. After my attempt to clean my cell, I lied down and closed my eyes but once again a voice disturbed me, "Simon how are ya man"? A voice asked. I quickly sat up and in the door stood Samuel, he was covered in grime and reeked, he smiled and decaying one, and laughed when I became wide eyed. I walked to him, "wow Samuel, you look . . . . well you look like you've been buried". I laughed. He smiled, and looked at his clothes which were now rags, torn and dirty, he chuckled, "wow your right". He replied. I chuckled and smiled, he looked at me quickly, "so what's happened since I've been gone"? He asked gravely. I sighed and lay back, "well I'm now at the top of the food chain, everyone is looking at me like I'm some bad ass prison thug, because of that whole Calvin thing". I replied slowly. He sighed, "Well it doesn't seem that bad . . . . I looked at him shocked, "are you kidding ever since he died the inmates are trying to kill me"? I replied in frustration. He nodded and sat down, "well I'm back little man so I've got our back, don't worry you wont get killed, your to popular now". He chuckled. "Yeah but being popular not only makes them more hostile but more focused on killing me". I said hastily. He chuckled, "well I'll have you know Simon, and this is your fight for the finish". He laughed. "Devil" I Corrected, he flashed me a look of confusion, "what"? I slowly scratched my head "devil, that's what goblin and the inmates call me now". I sighed. He nodded, "devil . . . huh, what a name goblin gave you that name?" He asked slowly. "Yeah why is that bad"? I quickly asked. He smiled and sighed, "No not bad just weird, goblin has been in here for twenty years he is a loner but respected". He replied. I smiled, "what'd he do"? I asked curious. He flopped down beside me and stared up at the ceiling, "well I'm not exactly sure but supposedly he robbed a bank and had sixteen hostages all kids on a field trip he killed two". I looked at him wide eyed, "wow that's crazy". I said under my breath. "So devil huh that's a neat name". He smiled and patted is back, "yep devil, that's me". I snorted. He sighed and lied back on the bed, "should you like change or something"? I asked quickly. He opened his eyes and laughed, "oh Simon, I would if had an available shower and clean clothes, but it would seem that I'm shit out of luck". He replied then closed his eyes again. "Do you like goblin"? I quickly asked. He opened one eye, "I duno, now shut up". He replied in a hostile way. I sighed and jumped on the top bunk and closed my eyes. I dreamt of rose and the twins, and how they would look once I got out of this place.

Chapter 10

the escape

Dear Samuel as you can tell I'm not here, I'm leaving this place once and for all even if I get caught or shot, I don't care, I no longer can live like this. By the time you finish this note I'll hopefully be in London, I'm going to find my family and fix the wrong I have done, I'm sorry I up and left you so suddenly, but if I don't go now I never will I'm glad I met you you're an amazing guy.

P.S. once you're done reading this note, please destroy it.

Sincerely: Simon Lucre, (aka devil)

The first night that I escaped I hid in an old abandoned barn, and to my surprise I didn't get found. I knew I was wanted now and everyone would be looking for me so I had to think of a way to disguise myself and fast. I dyed my hair a black and found some old clothes from a bum on the side of the street so while he was sleeping I snatched them and changed, I kept my old clothes though, and I tucked them in an old bag which I also took from the bum. I must have walked for hours to the train, and once I found it I nearly chocked I would jump the train and go to London, once there I would find rose and my children and I would make everything right again. I slept behind a bag of barley in the last cart, it was cold and the snow was falling in large clumps, covering the world in a fine blanket of snow, by then the earth had become a white wonderland. After several train jumps I arrived in London at around midnight; I slipped off the train and walked down the lonely streets. I rented a small apartment and the second I hit the bed I passed out. I awoke to the chirping of birds, and the roaring of vehicles I sat up and looked out the small window above the bed, the streets were bustling with Londoners, and snow covered everything masking the beautiful colored objects in ashen. I traveled the streets all day and asked everyone if they knew a woman named rose, or the twins. They all shook their heads no and walked away. By the end of the day I was overflowing with frustration, no mater how hard I looked no mater how many people I asked I couldn't locate her or my kids. Once I was back in my lodging, I sat on my bed and cried, I was out of prison finally and in London but I couldn't find my family and it tore me apart, the owner of the apartment complexes I was in was a short fat an with a long beard, he had silvery eyes and every time he looked at me I received chills down my spine and an unbearable nocuous feeling, so I dodged his looks and strayed clear of him and his stares. When I awoke the snow had ceased leaving London in a white blinding mess, that day I once again searched for rose, I received an address from the local tailor, and so I went to the location to find an old white Victorian house with red shutters and stone steps, so I gradually walked to the door and knocked. "Coming" A voice screamed and as it slipped through my ears I instantly knew it was rose, then in seconds the door opened and in a white gown standing clear as glass was rose. She gasped at my sight and pulled me into her, "Simon, oh my god". She gasped. But was interrupted by another voice, "who is it rose"? It asked. I quickly backed away, "who is that"? I demanded. She sighed and smiled her famous sexy smile, "Henry come here I want you to meet someone". She called. A tall older man walked up to her, "Henry this is Simon, the twin's father". She laughed. His eyes grew wide, and he stuck out his hand, "wow! It's so nice to finally meet you, come in please". He laughed. "Who is here mommy'? A small voice called. And standing on the bottom stair was my precious Edith, her hair was shoulder long black as night, and two crystal blue eyes shined from her ivory face. "Edith, go get your brother" rose replied. She nodded and ran up the stairs. And in less than a second, Edgar trotted down the stairs, he to had mid night hair, but instead of blue eyes he had two brilliant silver eyes. I gasped at the sight. Edith, Edgar would you both please come into the living room". She instructed. They smiled and did as she said. "Kids I have something to tell you, so sit down and listen". They giggled and sat down. "This is Simon; you know how when you were really small we moved here and you always asked about your daddy well Simon is your daddy". She said slowly. Their eyes widened and their jaws dropped, Edgar stood up first and slowly walked towards me, I sat in silence I was so nervous, "you re not my dad"? He said bitterly. I looked at him in shock, "Edgar I am your father". I replied he looked at rose then to me "my dad's dead". He bellowed then ran up stairs. Roses face went white and her jaw dropped, "Edgar you come down here right now". She screamed I sighed and looked at her sadly, "don't bother he hates me". I replied. Edith stood feet away she just stared at me with an expressionless face, and then looked at rose, "mom is it true is he our dad"? She asked doubtfully, rose nodded and looked at me with sad eyes, little Edith walked towards me and held out her hand, "it's finally nice to meet you Simon". She smiled. By then the twins were eight, and rose and Henry allowed me to stay with them for as long as it took for me to get situated. The fact of rose with Henry made me sick to my stomach, so I immediately took her to the side, "how long have you two been together"? I asked angrily. She sighed, "Please Simon, do not do this right now, I haven't the time". She cried. I looked at her quickly, "I thought you'd wait for me rose". I replied in frustration. She flashed me a glare, "what you thought I'd wait for you, just sit here and hope that some day you'd come back to us and everything would be the way it was"? She asked surprised. "Simon it's been six years, six long years". She cried I quickly sighed, "I just thought you'd wait for me, not go and get someone else to replace me". I screamed. "Replace you! Do you actually think that's what this is? How dare you, what was I suppose to do just put my life on hold, you know what your so damn selfish". She yelled. "That's not what I mean rose" I retaliated. She rolled her eyes and glared at me. "Well what did you mean then Simon"? She asked hurriedly. I sighed, "I just thought that when I got out, we would be a family still, not you fucking some old creep". I screamed. "Screw you Simon, he isn't a creep I love him Simon, is that a crime". "You know what Simon for once in your fucked up life is it possible for you to think of someone besides yourself, you selfish bastard"?

She screamed. "Me selfish, are you serious, if it's anyone who is selfish it's you, during those brief months we were married, it was always about you, you, you, you". I replied now in anger "oh please Simon, don't even start, while we were married which for your information was three years, it was nowhere near all about me, mostly about you and your fucked up desire for slaughtering younger girls, don't think I forgot about that". She screamed. "Oh please rose, you knew what I was doing, and you didn't even try to stop me once, you're just as fucked up as I am". I replied bitterly. "Your right Simon I knew, I knew all along, and I didn't try to stop you, you want to know why? It's because I didn't want you to come home and slit my throat, I was afraid of you and all the shit you were doing". I laughed, "Scared! Are you serious if you were so fucking scared then why didn't you leave me sooner"? I asked nastily. She was in tears by then, "because I loved you Simon, I loved you so much, you were everything to me, all I had". She cried. And I that brief moment she was back in my arms, she pulled my face to hers and kissed me forcefully, "oh Simon, I love you so much, I've waited for so long for this moment". She cried then kissed me again. By then I had her pushed up against the wall, tearing off her blouse, kissing her all over, "I crave you so badly rose". I cried. I quickly backed away, "what about Henry"? I quickly asked. Her eyes opened wide, and she shrugged her shoulders "follow me". She instructed she then brought me to an old play house, she pulls me to the ground and pushes me down she climbs on top and kisses my neck, I am waiting dying loosing it quickly, she smiles her fingers dance down she hold me with firmness and starts to pull and tug she is laughing, I close my eyes and pull her under me, I do not go inside of her instead I kiss her, my tongue dances across her lips, I suck her and gently bite at her my tongue inserts her she screams and bucks up I push her down and insert my finger one then two in and out she moans and gasps her body falls loose and I smile, she climaxes and I go no more, the windows fogged up and moans escaped our mouths. I gently kissed her forehead. I sighed, "Rose I'm sorry about all the things I said, I didn't mean any of it I swear". I whispered. She smiled and kissed me again, "I know Simon, and I didn't mean any of what I said either". "What about Henry"? I asked. "What about him"? She quickly replied. "Well how is this going to work"? "I don't understand Simon, how is what going to work"? She asked in confusion "me and you". Her eyes grew wide, "it isn't Simon, and we are not getting back together". I looked at her shocked, "what the hell rose, I thought you loved me, I thought you wanted us to be together". "No Simon I never said that". I looked at her now completely frustrated, "well I assumed that this whole thing was us getting together". I screamed. "Simon I have a life right now, I have Henry and I love him and he loves me". She replied hastily. "Then what was this? What happened in this room"? I demanded. "Sex Simon, that's what happened, nothing special". I looked at her in disbelief, "you are such a whore rose, how dare you, so you just felt like it and what I just happened to be available"? She chuckled quickly, "get over it Simon, what you actually thought I saved myself for you? Are you that stupid"? She asked in laughter. I quickly stood up, "I don't know why I even wasted my time with you, I can't even describe how much I hate you right now rose, and frankly I could slaughter you right now and not even care". I screamed in rage. Her eyes grew wide, "are you fucking threatening me Simon, is that what you're actually doing, seriously you come into my home and for some fucked up reason I actually allow you to see your kids and you threaten me, if I were you I'd watch what the hell you say"? She replied in fury. I smiled "I don't know rose, is that what it sounds like"? I chuckled. "I have to go Simon, and if I were you I'd watch what you say to me or Henry because frankly I hate you right now". She quickly stuttered than stood up, "what are you afraid"? I laughed. "Afraid! Are you kidding, what is their to be afraid of, you wont hurt me I know you to well besides you don't have the guts for it". She laughed then slowly headed for the door. I quickly snatched her by the arm, "do you want to bet on that rose"? I demanded hastily. She quickly pulled her arm away, "don't you ever touch me Simon, I don't want your blood stained hands anywhere near me". She screamed.

"Well that wasn't what you were thinking when we were having sex, you dumb whore". I replied. By then she had left and was already on the porch. That night I prowled the streets for my new prey to slaughter, one that resembled rose I searched and searched and when I found her I nearly fainted, she was identical from the blonde curly hair down to the blue eyes, she was perfect and I needed her. So as planned I followed her she stopped in the middle of the bridge, so I cunningly snuck up behind her and bashed her over the head she fell with grace and didn't make a sound, I became numb as she hit the pavement, I laughed in glory and my body tingled and my sex hardened. I slowly drug her body to the alley way and ripped her clothes off, revealing her ivory skin and perfect body, I was so angry at that point I didn't care how messy I was I cut her into pieces and laughed the entire time I hated rose and I hated life I wanted so badly to rip her into a thousand pieces I carved S and L into her chest and left her exposed for all to see. At that I gathered myself and left. I rushed to my apartment and cleaned myself; I quickly showered and destroyed my clothes. I slept a little that night but the face of that girl swam in my mind, and the thought of me taking her life made me boil with guilt and self sickness. 'Why did I do that? Why did I kill her, why was I jeopardizing my life and freedom?' those questions buzzed in my skull and made me vomit in my mouth. But in a sense I knew why I did it because if I didn't kill that girl I would have went back to that house and slaughtered rose in a heart beat but then again I so badly wanted to take it back I wanted to just walk by her and not touch her, but I did I killed her and to make matters worse I put my signature on her corpse, the morning came abruptly and once the sun rose I got dressed and went out, I had to act normal, very normal, so I had some coffee and read the paper, but the latest report made me nervous.

Last night the body of Cameron Eugene was found, she was brutally murdered on her way home to her children, two entitles were carved into her chest, S and L. it would seem that the serial killer is back and once again we recommend you to stay indoors at night, to further prevent any more killings'.

I slowly sipped my coffee and acted as if I had no clue of whom had or would do this horrid act, but the part of her returning home to her children, made me sick, I quickly doubled over and threw up on the pavement, a few customers looked at me quickly and stood up, "sir are you ok"? They asked in concern. I nodded then left. I rushed home at once and went to bed, I was the most inhumane person on planet earth and there was nothing I could do to fix it, I sulked in self pity and threw up every second. I made a pact to myself that night that I would never take the life of another human again and that if I did I would end myself instantly and without hesitation. I grabbed a taxi and went to see the twins, but when I arrived at the gate I noticed there were two cop cars parked in her driveway, so I told the driver to turn around and drop me off at the apartment. The second I arrived at the apartment I packed my belongings and headed to the train station, I jumped a train and stayed in the last cart, I jumped off the train in Ireland.

Chapter 11

ireland the new beginning

Green meadows and bright flowers greeted me, I made my way to Dublin, their I found a small cottage to live in for a low price, I worked on the nearby farm herding cattle and sheep, I made a hourly wage of ten dollars every three hours, so I made an effort to work a twenty four hour day, so I made eight dollars a day so two hundred and forty dollars a month, which wasn't that bad. I mad several friends and lived a great life and as of today I had been in Ireland for over three years. Her name was Elizabeth, she had green emerald eyes, fiery red hair and ivory skin, and she was beautiful, like a goddess. She moved in with me and it wasn't long before I proposed to her and she said yes without hesitation. Our wedding was amazing, it was held in green meadow flowers enclosing us. She wore a brilliant white gown, roses entangled in her hair. But since I came to Ireland roses face stayed in the back of my mind I thought about her all the time I wanted her back but I knew deep inside of my heart she hated me and never wanted to see my sickening face ever again I no longer worked on the farm but instead got a job in the local market slicing and selling beef and sheep. We lived a simple glorious life Elizabeth and I, and it wasn't long before we had a beautiful baby girl, we named her Aurora, she had green eyes and red curly hair like her mother, she was a miracle the very definition, she was an angel Elizabeth's and I's angel. Her first birthday was held in the same green meadow, Elizabeth made her a white layered cake, I bought her a golden locket with me and her mothers face inside, Elizabeth bought her dolls and had a white playhouse built for her, inside everything a normal house had, made of the cherry wood. She loved it and played in it every waking hour, her dolls lined up at her miniature table, where she frequently hosted tea parties for them. The first few months went by great but one day I came home to find Elizabeth in bed a doctor leaning over her, she had come down with some disease I don't know what actually but it was eating away at her immune system leaving her weak and near death and the doctors claimed she was hardly hanging on, I prayed for her every day and took a couple of days off to tend to her. Elizabeth died a month later, and I had her buried under a weeping willow in the back yard a white tombstone with an angel hands in a prayer form. I cried every night after and my heart felt like it had torn in pieces, I wanted her back so badly I wanted to spend more time with her take her on walks and make her laugh what I would do to get her back. Aurora didn't seem to take a big toll on her death and for that I was thankful, but once in a while she would ask when her mommy was coming home, I would pull her to me and comfort her. I would tell her that her mommy was in heaven looking down on us everyday every night we would kneel and say a prayer for Elizabeth, as months passed and years took their place, aurora started school and she seemed to be quite warmhearted of it, and in no time she had a party of friends mostly small girls I allowed her to have sleep over's and she hosted tea parties for them just like she did with her dolls. It warmed my heart knowing she was happy and I did everything in my power to make her happier no mater the cause or difficulty. I loved her and treasured her more than life itself; she was my angel and my goddess. By then she had grown into a fine young lady red curls enclosed her emerald luminous eyes and ivory fair skin, she was a mature thirteen year old with the highest knowledge of life, loss and a heart filled to the rim with love. I can recall when she came home one day and told me that she had found the boy of her dreams named Lucas, and that he was the prefect man for her. I asked her to bring him over so that I could meet this lad, and when she did he was everything she bragged he was, he had short brown hair with hazel creamed eyes, and he was smart and had a plan for his future already. He had originally come from England France; he claimed that his father had moved him and his mother to Ireland seeking a job and a new life. I allowed her to date him on one exception that they were not to have sex or any other sexual contact, kissing and holding hands and dates was fine but not sex, at least not ever in my house and never to my knowledge. They must have dated for a month then broke up, she came home in tears and sobs, I asked her immediately what had happened she only cried harder, and she said that she caught him flirting with another girl. I comforted her and ensured her that maybe she got the wrong idea, but she looked at me in rage, "he kissed her daddy, I saw them kiss". She cried. I sighed and pulled her close, "aurora don't get hung up over this guy, there are plenty fish in the sea, you just wait one day you'll find someone who will make your heart jump". I replied. She wiped her eyes and smiled, "is that how you felt when you meet mom"? She asked shyly. I nodded, "exactly your mother stuck out to me like a sore thumb, and the second I laid eyes on her I knew she was the one". I said slowly almost in tears. I didn't sleep that night I was too fretful, for what I'm unsure but my body was throbbing my bones ached and I was masked deep in uneasiness I just couldn't keep at rest, Aurora slept on the couch in my room that night she was still upset about her break up. I must have stayed up until six in the morning I cleaned the house from top to bottom I cleaned until my fingers bled, my knees were blistered from kneeling the entire time and my skin had been burned in several spots from the deep cleaners I was using. It was around ten in the morning when I received a bang on the door, I quickly leaped up and answered it, and in my doorway stood that whore of a mother I had. I just stared at her, she looked tired and grim, her hair was matted and hung at clumps at her shoulders, she was old so old her face was wrinkly and her eyes were red and dead beat looking she didn't smile of make any sort of facial expression just complete emptiness, and she was dressed in what seemed to be her pajamas. By then aurora had left for school leaving me alone for a few hours before I had to go to work She glanced down at my hands with her sullen eyes and sighed, as I noticed this I quickly folded my hands behind my back and looked at her in anguish "what are you doing here mother, why are you in Ireland and how did you find me"? I demanded cynically. She just fiddled with her fingers and then sighed lifting her head up and staring into my eyes she said "you've been up to no good son, no good you've been up to no good son, no good" she repeated this several times like some broken recorder. I backed up quickly, hoping she would follow me inside, but she just stood in the same spot, her eyes bulging and her lips muttering the same thing. I was beckoning her in, I so badly just wanted her to step inside my house so I could just swat her like the fly she was. She smiled then and looked at me, "I love you Adam". She spewed. "I really do, Adam don't you love me"? She asked. I just looked at her and gasped she too had forgotten who I was. I looked at her, and by then I was in a fit of rage, "how dare you call me Adam, I'm not Adam you fool I'm Simon, now get out"!!!! I screamed. Her eyes grew dangerously wide and a smile played across her lips, "oh son, you are surly mistaken, you are not Simon, you're my Adam, my sick little son, Adam that's who you are"!! I just stared at her in disbelief, "you lie, you lie, you lie, and you lie". I screamed. She quickly lurched forward and pulled me back by my shirt, "oh but you are my Adam, my little Adam, you're a devil a sinner a bad apple, but you are my Adam never the less". Blood rushed to my face and my body went numb I quickly punched her in the head and shoved her back, "you liar, get out of my house, you come here and lie to me, get out" I screamed. She just smiled and stood there, "oh Adam, please understand that I'm not leaving you here, oh Adam, that's who you are Adam, you're still so sick my baby boy so sick, I just want you to get better that's all my Adam that's all". Her voice by then was slowly increasing getting higher and higher to a full scream. That's when I felt it, my body began to tremble, my feet started to twitch and the hairs on the nape of my neck rose and I felt cold, as if I had instantly turned to ice. Mother was standing beside me then, and I was on the ground, my senses dulled and my eyes felt like lead, and when I finally managed to open them she was gone. I quickly sat up and looked around; I questioned myself all-night whether or not I had imagined the entire episode with mother 'was I Adam? Was I living a lie?' 'Of course not, that would be stupid and impossible' I assured myself of these things but that's when I heard it a sudden clicking, ticking, the instant mumbling and whining and the screaming, the heavy footsteps that followed, the loud thuds and boom's.

Chapter 12

back to reality

My chest burned and I immediately started to vomit, and once again I awoke in the hospital, "Adam, Adam are you ok'? A voice demanded, I quickly looked ahead and in front of my stood the girl from the bar, the one I buried. A gasp rolled out of my mouth and I froze, 'this wasn't happening'. I thought. I looked at her, "who am I"? I asked calmly. She sighed, "well your Adam, you silly goose, why what is wrong"? She asked surprised. I looked at her, "No! I'm Simon you fool, why would you call me that"? I demanded. She quickly took a step back, "Now Adam, you had better stop this right now, Simon is in the waiting room, with your mother and father, and if you want to see them you had better stop it"! With that she left. 'They were dead all of them, mother that girl Adam, and soon mother'. The same girl came in and smiled at me, so now Adam, would you like to see them now"? She asked in a sharp voice. I slowly nodded my head and then closed my eyes, hoping that this was all a dream. She slowly left the room, but when the door opened once more I gasped and nearly screamed, and in

117

walked Adam, and to my surprise he was young, very young. Mother and father followed right behind. "hi Adam!' they all sang at the same time. I looked at them and quickly shot out of the bed, "GO AWAY—GO AWAY"!! I screamed. Father approached me, "son how are you doing"? He asked in his usual mono—tone voice. I quickly backed away, "your dead, you're all dead, all of you go away"! I screamed while smacking my head, trying to wake up. Father quickly stepped back, "Adam why do you say these things? We love you and we have been here for you all along". He muttered, distress playing across his face. wrath by now had completely filled my body 'I wanted to just wake up' Adam came forth then tried to hug me but I quickly shoved him back, "don't you touch me, your dead your all dead, not here none of you are here, not here, not here" I muttered repeating myself. By then the faces of the dead looked shocked and sad, "Adam we don't understand, aren't you happy to see us"? They all asked. I just stared at them, "you don't even remember my name, your all stupid stop calling me Adam, I'm not Adam, I'm Simon your son, Simon, that's who I am, don't you remember"? I wasn't really asking I was begging, 'how could they just forget who I am?, and how was it possible I was even having this conversation with them'? I was now on the threshold of tears, I just wanted to wake up, and have everything back to normal, where dead people stayed dead and back to my lovely daughter that's all I wanted was it to much to ask for? Mother was in front of me then, and I hadn't even bothered to back away, I was in shock. "Son, I think you just need to calm down"! She said smiling. I looked at her, "calm down, don't you see your all dead I killed every one of you, your just screwing with my head, that's all, it's just a dream, a bad dream and when I wake it will all be ok". I assured myself of this. Ten they all came closer, "oh Adam you're so sick, so, so sick, we can help you, you just have to let us my sick, sick boy, oh my Adam". Mother cried. I looked at them in hate, "SICK? I AM NOT SICK, IT'S ALL OF YOU WHO ARE SICK, NOT ME"! I screamed, my voice giving out at the end. I was in a fit of tears by then, sobbing like a baby. They all looked at me, and at once mother and father came forth, "oh Adam, why do you do this to us"? They asked. I looked at them and backed away. "Oh Adam don't you know we love you, we love you so much, don't you know that"? I looked at them and hate circled through me, "stop calling me Adam, I'm not Adam". I cried. Mother was in tears by then and father was cradling her, "son, just stop, can't you see that your only hurting yourself by telling yourself these lies, you are not Simon you are Adam just wake up"? He yelled in an angry voice. Mother was staring at me, "son, won't you just open your eyes, can't you just stop this act, and see what you're doing to us"? She pleaded in a half cry. Father looked at me, "son you fell, and don't you remember you were on the ice and you slipped and you got hurt". He said in a low voice. I looked at him "what"? He looked at me and straightened up, "son it was on Christmas and you were playing on the pond, we told you to stay away but you didn't listen and you fell through the ice, you were hurt so we took you to the hospital, and from their you just started to believe you were Simon, so we were forced to bring you here". He said in a sympathetic voice. I looked at him, "father don't you see I am Simon, and that's impossible I've lived here in London for half my crazy life and then Ireland, cant you see that what you're saying cant be factual, I have a job I have kids . . . it's just not plausible". I spewed my voice gradually increasing. Father sighed, "Oh son, that can't be you've been here all along in this hospital". He said in a reassuring tone. "What hospital"? I demanded. He just stared at me for several seconds, "in the mental hospital, why you forgot"? He asked in a serious tone. I looked at him, "you lie, why would I be here, I've done no wrong"? I screamed. Father sighed, 'oh Adam, you are such a great boy, but like I said you started to act weird and like now you started calling yourself Simon, and then you started hurting your brother, so we had to send you here, we had no choice". He muttered. I looked at him, "don't you remember that you sent me to stay with Aunt Bertines"? I pleaded. He shook his head, "why would you say that, your aunt has been deceased for several years". He said angrily. I looked at mother and father and ran to the door, only to find it was locked, father was beside me then, "son please just sit down, so we can talk". He said bitterly. "Why are you guys doing this to me, why are you being this way, what wrong have I done to deserve this cruel punishment?" I asked, in tears for a second time. After my last attempt to tell them the reality of the situation they left. I was alone that night and I was miserable, I just couldn't see how this was happening to me, I know Adam was dead and so was the girl from the bar, I killed them, I watched the blood pore, and I saw the dead bodies. Was I crazy, did I dream the entire thing? I was restless all night and when the sun rose I was drenched in fear, it wasn't long before my door opened and a tall black man wearing a white coat walked in, in his large hands was a clip board. "Morning young man, how are you feeling today"? He asked in a high deep voice. I looked at him, "who am I "? I asked in desperation. He eyed me closely, "Now Adam you know very well who you are, so if I were you I'd stop this game". He said insistently. He then took a bottle of pills out of his coat pocket and handed it to me, "take your meds Adam". He ordered. I looked at him sadly, and then took two "three Adam you take three". He said in anger. I quickly snatched the bottle out of his hand and took three. "There I took three, now can I go"? I asked in irony. He smiled. "Young man you need to stop playing games with me, if you don't straighten your shit I'll take you to the pads". He informed then stuffed the pill bottle in his pocket. "Pad what pads?" I asked quickly. His eyebrow pulled in close and he let out a snarl, "I warned you Adam, but you just don't listen". At that he pulled me out of the room by my shirt. And before I knew it I was tied up in some shirt with my arms wrapped around my waist and stuck inside a padded room. "Please let me out, I demand to know what I did wrong". I screamed. But I wasn't answered. I was in that room for hours and I desperately had to go pee, and to soil myself would be childish so I held it. "Please let me out I'm sorry, I have to pee please". I begged. I was finally answered about an hour later by the same black man, "Are you going to stop your crap Adam"? He demanded. By then had nearly swallowed my tongue, "I did no wrong sir, if you let me out know I won't mention this to the authorities". I replied smugly. He chuckled, "go ahead no one's stopping you Adam tell . . . tell the world go ahead yell". He laughed. "Please let me out, I have to go pee, please sir I can't hold it anymore". I begged once more my legs wobbled and I just couldn't hold it anymore, and in an instant it all came out, warm at first but ended with a slight burn to my inner thighs. I watched as the floor filled with my yellow waste, slowly soaking into the floor pads. He just stood at the door staring at me through the small barred window, disgust filled his face and he shook his head then left me to suffer their. Later on through the day I found out that the long shirt I was put into was called a straight jacket, and the room I was trapped in was called solitary, the main purpose of the room and jacket was to make the victim struggle while thinking about the wrong that the individual had preformed. I must have been in that room for at least two to three days soiling myself when I no longer had the will to hold it in. when I was finally let out I was give the chance to take a bath, supervised by a woman employer. After my soaking I was brought to smaller room, I no longer had to wear the straight jacket instead was given a pair of dark grey pants with a teal short sleeved shirt. I changed then supervised by a woman who surprisingly wore a light pink shirt with printed flowers all over it she too carried a clipboard, with Adam written on top. I looked at her then and in a low voice asked why the name on the clipboard was Adam. She looked at me with a slight smile, "well Adam what would you like to be called"? She asked in a weary smile. I sighed and kicked the ground, "how about Simon"? I sang instantly. Her eyes grew dangerously wide "do you want me to go get Mr. chides"? She threatened through clenched teeth. I sighed, "Who is mister Chide"? I asked hastily. She shook her head, "the man from earlier, he's black". She informed. Fear ran down my body and I nearly started to cry, "oh no please no" I cried in terror. Her face went white and she took my hand into hers, "oh Adam he isn't that bad . . . is he"? "He put me in that room, and . . . and watched me soil myself". I replied in a hushed tone. She sighed, "Well if you are a good little boy and stop calling yourself Simon, then I promise you that you won't ever have to see that room again". As she said this her chin rose and she started for the door, but paused as she was about to leave, "Adam might I ask you a question"? She asked. I sighed, "sure anything". I replied. She smiled kindly, "why do you think you are Simon"? She asked quickly. I looked at her in a strange way, and in that single moment I knew she feared me and all that I represented, to her I was poison my presence horrifying, and I automatically knew what an awful person she was. "Because I am Simon, I just don't understand why you and everyone lately keep calling me Adam, I'm not him, he is a vile self centered person, it's almost like you and the world totally forgot who I am". I replied sadly. She left then her face sullen and confused. I just couldn't grasp why everyone around me were still playing their games, it was ripping me apart what had I done that was so horrid that I had to live like this? I slept at ease that night, and to no surprise the breakfast was dreadful I was brought to the cafeteria or what they called it the 'eating place', it was a dull place, and once I actually looked around, I noticed the room was filled with little kids, kids my size, and I nearly choked at the sight of it, but to be honest my gaze was directed to a small girl with blonde curls and blue eyes, and the moment I saw her face I almost fainted, it was rose, my rose I finally had her back. The first day in the cafeteria I sat alone and was frequently stared at, I knew they were talking about me behind my back, and it bugged me so badly. I later found out that her name was charlotte, but no matter her name she was my rose, my life and all that was ever important to me. I was in devastation by the end of the day, I didn't do anything and no one talked to me or even attempted, during recreational time I sat alone and stared out the window, we weren't allowed outside. When night fell and I had to go back to my room the small bed was uncomfortable and I felt ill, and all I could think about was charlotte, I wanted to talk to her but in a way I was scared to, scared that by some chance I might say the wrong thing and that she would never want to talk to me again, just like rose had. Each day consisted of eleven hours; we woke at seven, had lunch at eleven and dinner at three then went to bed at six. We could either watch black n white TV, usually cartoons or we could play board games and puzzles, or on special occasions we were allowed outside to play in the sand box or on the merry-go-round. I approached charlotte rather slowly at first; I told her my name and asked her if she wanted to be my friend. At first she looked at me like I was a retard or something. Mother and or father hadn't come during the first three months and in a way I was happy but also sad during that time I had made several attempts to break free resulting into me being tied up in the jacket and thrown into the pads, I'd only spent at lest a week or two before I no longer minded it, sure being all tied up cramped my arms but I was alone and everything was quiet. I believe it's my birthday today, all the nurses are being really nice to me, nicer than usual, mother and father stopped by today, so I think it really is my birthday, they also brought some boxes which were wrapped in bright colored paper topped with bows. I wasn't allowed to open them, and when I found out I nearly screamed, like they brought them for me knowing I wasn't allowed to even look what was inside. I neatly stacked them under my bed and went to the recreational room and sat down. And right as I became comfortable a taller black haired boy came at me and pulled me off the chair, I looked at him quickly, "what is your problem"? He just smiled and kicked my leg, "this is my seat ugly face".

He laughed. I was in his face and I pushed him back, "I was here first". I screamed. He smiled, "are you going to cry, ugly face"? He teased. By then I was in rage and from head to toe was on fire. I quickly swung at his face and to my surprise I hit him, square in the nose, I watched as blood drizzled out and he fell to the floor and started to cry like a baby. Seconds later Mr. Chide and two other doctors came in and looked at him then to me, "Adam what happened"? Chide demanded. I sniffled, "he kicked me, I was sitting their first and he pulled me out of the chair and called me names". I replied. He nodded; the boy by then wasn't crying anymore but was standing up with a towel over his nose. Chide looked to him, "what happened, did you start this john"? He asked through clenched teeth. He quickly shook his head, "he punched me because I was in his seat". He lied. Chide looked at me in disappointment, "Adam are you lying to me"? He demanded. The out of know where a small voice butted in, "I saw what happened. Mr. Chide, john started it, he was calling Adam ugly face and kicked him". It said. And charlotte popped out from behind the couch. Chide looked at me then to her then to john, "ok I will take you word for it, take john to the pads". He instructed then walked away. Charlotte was at me side by then, she smiled and I badly wanted to kiss her one more time. "Why did you do that for me"? I quickly asked. She smiled, "because john is mean, and he doesn't need to call you names". She replied. I nodded, "thank you charlotte, you're nice to me". I replied. She chuckled and took my hand in hers, "what happened to your face Adam"? She asked in a low voice. I looked at her confused, "what do you mean"? I asked quickly now alarmed. She smiled, "never mind Adam, so why are you here"? She asked quickly. I looked at her and sighed, "Because no one believes I'm Simon and not Adam". I said slowly. She gave me an uncomfortable look, "really I'm sorry, do you want me to call you Simon"? She asked suddenly. I smiled, "no I might get in trouble, why are you in here"? I asked back. She looked at the ground and fiddled with her fingers, "when I lived with my mommy, I did a bad thing, she was on the couch sleeping and I was hungry and I had to wake her so I found a jug of water and I poured it on her face, it wasn't water Adam, it hurt my mommy it made her face ugly so she took me here, she doesn't love me anymore and when I get out I'm going to live with my grandma". As she was saying this she was crying and I felt awful for asking. I later found out that charlotte had been in here for three years and she would be leaving very soon, and when I actually gathered this information I started to cry, right when I found her again she would be leaving. When it was finally time for bed, I didn't sleep I just lye in that uncomfortable bed and stared up at the ceiling. I was sent to the pads at lunch today and frankly I don't know why, I spent three hours in their and was let out at dinner, that's when I noticed charlotte was no where to be found, I looked and looked and finally asked the supervisor Mr. Thomas, I asked where she was and when she would be coming back to eat, but he only patted my back and smiled, "charlotte was released this morning" he said slowly. I looked at him hurt, "why?" I begged. He smiled, "Adam it was her time, she is better now much better". He replied. I looked at him shocked, "where did she go, her mommy doesn't love her anymore"? I asked quickly, hoping he would say something to put me at ease. He sighed and flashed me a dirty look, "Go eat Adam, and shut your mouth". He instructed. I sighed, "You don't have to yell at me, I was only asking". I replied in a low voice. He mumbled something and pushed me in the line for food. Dinner that night consisted of potatoes a roll and some pre cut meat, I didn't eat it though I was to sad, I felt so alone again, I loved that girl and now she was gone. The rest of the day I just sat on the couch in the recreational room, I didn't move talk or do much of anything, charlotte was gone and now I was all alone, how could she just leave me like that?, she was my friend and she still left and for it I hated her. When the bell for bed rang I didn't move, and my eyes instantly filled with tears, one of the supervisors found me her name was Mrs. Scheme, came to me and sat beside me but I hardly noticed, "Adam your mom and dad are coming tomorrow". She informed. I didn't say anything or move so she pulled me close to her, "Adam why so sad"? She asked in a sympathetic voice. I wiped my tears away and looked at her, "charlottes gone, and now I have no friends". I cried. She sighed and patted my back, "oh Adam it'll be ok, you just wait you'll find another friend". She assured. But I shook my head and started to cry again, "I don't think that's possible, she was special to me". I replied gasping. She smiled and kissed my head, "you just wait and see Adam, and friends are plenty in the world, now it's time for bed". She replied and escorted me to my room. She stopped as she was about to close the door, "how are you Adam"? She asked in concern I smiled kindly, "I'm ok I guess, but I can't sleep anymore". I said slowly. She smiled, "ill talk to the doctor tomorrow and we'll see what we can do about that". With that she left. I didn't sleep that night and it wasn't a surprise to me, I was too anxious for morning why I have not a clue, mother and father showed up at about noon, and I was in the recreational room when Mrs. Scheme pulled me out.

Mother father and Adam were sitting on large yellow couch in the talking room when I showed up, I sat down across from then and when Mrs. Scheme left I stood up but mother was already by my side, she went to hug me but I pushed her away and approached Adam, "so how are you Simon"? I asked sarcastically. He flinched and made an ugly face, "you're no brother of mine". He yelled. I started to laugh then, he feared me and I envied it, he was afraid of the sight of me, I could sense it feel it in my bones, his legs shook and sweat balled on his forehead. Mother came to me and gently wrapped her arms around my shoulders but I pushed her away, "don't you touch me ever again". I warned. She backed away and wiped her eyes, "Adam, what is wrong"? She demanded. I shook my head in disgust, "why do people stare at me all the time, why do they make faces at me and call me ugly face"? I demanded. She must have swallowed her tongue because she was silent for several minutes. She slowly sat down and pulled me down beside her, "when you were small Adam you got hurt, you and Simon were on the pond you fell through the ice and cut your face from your eye down to your chin". She replied as she traced the scar. I flinched away quickly, "I don't believe you mother". I screamed. I turned my attention to Adam, "you little bastard, what did you do to my face, what did you do?" I screamed coming at him. He was at the door by then banging on it hastily "stay away, stay away from me"? He begged then fell to the floor. Mother had me by the forearm by then, "let me go, let me go you whore". I screamed. She quickly let go and I went foreword slipping and falling to the ground. "Now Adam you calm down right now, there is no need for this, your brother didn't do anything to you". She assured. "Look what he did to my face mother, but you still defend him, how dare you, how dare you, your no mother of mine and I hope you burn in hell you old miserable hag". I screamed. By then the room had flooded with doctors and supervisors, I was then bonded with the jacket and carried into the room. I spent an entire week in that room, they brought a meal to me at each feeding time. When I was finally let out, I didn't dare say anything to the doctors, I hated them and the world fare more. It was another week or two on which I received great news, the doctors said that if I straightened up and was a good little boy then I would be able to go home, but if I messed up once I would have to stay another year and then they would give me the same option. I was overjoyed when I heard this and in that second I nearly cried, but I held the tears back and smiled in a kind way, I would be on my best behavior until then, but while I was thinking about home and seeing my father, Adam came into mind, I knew I wouldn't be able to cope with him near by and the thought of it destroyed me once again, I wanted out of this place, but I also wanted to stay only because I never again wanted to see that retched Adam again, so if I did go home I would immediately kill that bastard and this time I would make absolute sure he was dead. I was so small to the world once again, and it bugged me knowing all my life's work had been destroyed by a simple act of reality; I just couldn't grasp the point of knowing that no one believed me still, and how they consistently called me Adam, ha! Me Adam, never I was much better then he would ever be, the things I saw in my life the things I did, the experiences I had, and while thinking about all of it, it still took my very breath away. And I knew that when I got out I would make everyone see the real me, the monster which was locked up and oh the so thrilling but sinful things I could accomplish. Never once did I see mother again, not after my break down that is, father on the other hand stopped in frequently, and at one point in time he brought me a piece of chocolate Dutch cake, which by the way was quite scrumptious. He sat with me for an hour or so and we talked about, what I would do once I got out, like school and sports, and friends, he was overjoyed as he said this and in a way so was I. it was on a Wednesday when I was scheduled to be released, I sat on the chair in the talking room, I was so happy I couldn't keep still, then mother walked in, and I knew in that instant I would explode, she always came at the wrong time. She slowly approached me but I just backed away, I wanted nothing to do with that wretched whore of a mother, she was a disease and when she touched anything it would shrivel up and perish. She smiled and kept coming foreword, "Adam my son, are you so happy to come home"? She asked in sarcasm. I didn't answer instead I ran the other way, "where's father, I want to see father". I said bitterly. Her eyes grew wide and she let out a deep sigh, "you father isn't coming, I'm here so lets go". She demanded crossly. I smiled, "I'm not going anywhere with you, I want father". I screamed. She quickly grabbed my arm and pulled me towards the door, but I didn't budge, I fought against her with all my might, I wasn't going anywhere with her, not now not ever. She let go and I fell to the ground with a thud, she let out a snarl, "you little shit, het your ass off that floor and lets go, I haven't all day Adam, your brother is in the car waiting so let's go". She screamed in frustration. I just sat their and shook my head, "no". I said calmly. "What did you say to me"? She demanded. I smiled, "I said no". I repeated. She quickly slapped me on the face, leaving my cheek burning like fire. I didn't cry though, I didn't even flinch, I wanted her to see that I wasn't afraid of her any longer, I wanted her to see that I no longer cared what she did to me. She raised her hand again and slapped me once more, but still I didn't wince or cry. She huffed in frustration and slapped me again, my cheek by then was throbbing and my nose was bleeding. She must have slapped me at least ten to eleven times, and after the last a doctor ran in and grabbed her hand. "Mrs. Lucre what on earth are you doing"? He demanded. By then she no longer was staring at me, instead her eyes were on the doctor. She let out a laugh and jerked her arm away, "fine you little piece of shit, and stay I don't care anymore you're no good to me alive or dead". She yelled then headed for the door, but was stopped by a police man; he smiled and tipped his hat, "Mrs. Lucre I'm officer brown, I understand that you've inflicted a great deal of abuse on this child here". He said notifying at me. Her eyes lit up and she sighed, "I don't know what you're talking about officer, I haven't touched that boy". She lied. He quickly looked at me and gave me a smile, "son be honest did she hurt you"? He asked. I looked at him then to mother, and in that instant I knew I had her, I nodded then started to fake cry. He nodded and walked towards mother, "Mrs. Lucre you're under arrest for child abuse on a mentally disabled person". He informed. She gasped, "He is not being honest officer, I did no such thing, now Adam you tell them the truth". She screamed. The officer just looked at her with pity, "Mrs. Lucre you have the right to trial by jury, you have the right to speedy and public trial, you have the right to an attorney, if you do not have an attorney you will be given one, do you understand the charges against you"? He asked. She looked at him with fury, "no officer so why don't you remind me". She said sarcastically. "You are being charged with child abuse". He said coolly. She smiled and looked at me, "I hate you Adam, and when I see you again I will end you". She threatened then was taken away, screaming down the halls like a mad man. The doctor came to me with a bag of ice, "are you ok Adam"? He asked in a meaningful way. I nodded, "what is going to happen to her"? I asked. He smiled, "nothing you need to worry about, your father is not answering his phone so you'll have to stay tonight, and hopefully by the morning all this will be worked out and you can go home, now she said your brother was still in the car right"? He asked. I nodded but with a great deal of hesitation, he smiled "well I'll have someone go get him; I guess he will have to stay here tonight as well". He informed. I choked at the thought of it, "he can't stay here doctor, and I don't want him around me". I mumbled. He looked at me shocked, "Adam he is your brother, just stop it". He scorned. And like minutes later Adam was inside the institute, he looked retched and the sight of him made me puke in my mouth. I slept in my same room and sadly he was in the same room, I didn't say a word to him, and when I did it was cruel and direct. He gave me a scared look when he entered the room; I looked at him and smiled, "so Simon, how are you and mother"? I asked out of the blue. He didn't answer for several minutes then his small voice cracked the silence, "ok, she's ok I guess". He replied. I nodded; he looked at me on the verge of tears, "Adam what's going to happen to mother"? He asked. I smiled and let out a sigh, "I don't know why does it matter anyway"? I asked sharply. He sighed and shrugged his shoulders, "Adam can I ask you something"? He questioned I nodded and sat down on my bed. "Why do you hate me so much"? He quickly mumbled. The question itself took my breath away, I didn't know how to answer "I don't hate you Simon, I merely don't like you that's all". I replied. He nodded and sat down beside me, "well why, don't you like me"? He asked shyly. To be frank I had never put thought to why I hated him so much so in a way it was hard to answer. I looked at him in deep thought. "Do you really want to know why"? I asked only to make sure he wanted to hear the truth which was about to spill from my mouth. He gave a simple nod and crossed his feet, "ok Simon, I don't like you because you have taken everything from me, you took father and mother and everything I ever wanted". I replied, I looked at him and he was crying tears spilling from his baby eyes. I patted him on the back, "there is no need to cry, you said you wanted me to be honest". I said quickly. He nodded and dried his tears, "I know, but Adam I don't understand how I did all that to you". He muttered slowly. I sighed, "it's quite easy really, before you were born mother and father were so happy, they were always playing with me and taking me out to random places to have fun, see Simon when you were born it all stopped they never once talked to me or praised me, it was all about you, you and your oh so cute eyes and your frizzy hair and your charming little voice, they forgot about me Simon, they never noticed I was even their anymore, it killed me inside Simon and you caused it, I know its not your fault being born and all, but you took everything from me, they gave my love to you". I replied slowly, I wanted him to understand what pain he brought me. He didn't say anything after I informed him he only sat and sulked crying for hours, "Adam I'm sorry you know, I never wanted any of that to happen, I love you I really do love you, not just because you're my brother but because you are my friend". He said slowly catching his breath every second. I looked at him in pity, "I know Simon, but it's hard for me to forgive you know, He sighed and quickly wrapped his arms around me, "Adam wont you please forgive me"? He begged but I just couldn't muster up the courage to even try. I quickly shook my head no and turned away from him. I hated him so much after what he did to me, after what he caused I would never be able to forgive him not now not ever, it just wasn't happening. Somehow during the night Simon came into the bed and when I woke he was beside me, all cuddled up to me and in an instant I was appalled. I quickly pushed him off the bed, he fell to the floor with a thud and looked at me through sleepy eyes, he didn't say anything just lied down on the cold floor and curled into a ball. I felt awful, I can say that much, I know how hard he tried last night to get me to forgive him, and me pushing him off the bed gave me a stomach full of guilt and self disgust. I looked at him and slowly pulled him back into the bed beside me, he turned towards me in alarm, "what are you doing Adam"? He asked slowly. I smiled and then pulled the blankets over him, "you can sleep with me Simon, I don't mind". I replied then closed my eyes and drifted off to sleep. When I woke up again I noticed I had my hands around Simons neck, shaking him viciously, the room was filled with doctors and several of them were trying me pull him away, I was staring into his eyes which were rolling all around he was gasping for breath and in a second I let go and he fell to the floor, I then was locked up in the pads bonded once again by the same jacket, I didn't understand how that happened, I must have had a bad dream and lashed out on him. Simon was taken to the E.R. and treated by several doctors, I knew he would be fine, and in reality I wasn't worried a bit about him, but mostly about myself, I had done it again I screwed up for the last time and I knew that I wasn't going anywhere not now not ever. Simon was immediately transferred to a foster home only because mother no longer was allowed to look over him and also because father was no where to be found. I guess the family he was moved to have a daughter and a little boy, I knew he would be much happier and probably less screwed up. I on the other had had just gotten out of the pads, I was immediately brought to the institutes physiatrist named Miss. Paulson she was a tall lady, skinny and neat, she asked me several questions none that I cared to answer, she babbled on and on about my sudden changes in mood and how I could control my tempers, she asked about why I disliked my brother so much and why I lashed out on him like that and what had caused it, I didn't know how to answer all of them so I just stayed mute, I was a zombie now, my insides throbbed and my heart stung, I was so screwed up, and I had just finally realized, and it damaged me knowing that I broke everything I touched, as in rose and my kids as in my father mother and Simon everything, and I made a vow to never touch anything ever again, I no longer wanted to be blamed for the wrong that happened I was way to tired and way to dead inside. I met with her everyday for an hour, it was only a waste of time though, and I knew she couldn't help me I was too screwed up for even an attempt. I hardly slept anymore just lied in my bed staring at the cracks in the ceiling knowing that this was my home for now and forever, I hated life and I desperately wanted out, but in an institute their was nothing to give me that way out, everything was made of plastic, no glass or metal like some plastic fortress to keep those of locked up tight to never see the sunrise or sunset again, no more clouds or the vast blue skies that rested above us. I longed for freedom but I also longed to stay here, out there was not for me, and in here was. Simon wrote me letters frequently, telling me about his new life and family, he loved it their and wished to never leave, and I knew that if I got out I to would be transferred to an orphanage to wait for some family to take me in and give the same love he was receiving. But I doubted it, who on earth would want me for a child, I was a monster and entirely unlovable, like some rock you passed by while walking in the park of some tree that lied on a farm decaying with time. I moped around the institute and never said a word to anyone, I never ate and never once had hope, how could I? seriously my life had no point now, the people I hurt the victims I slaughtered haunted me in my dreams, their ghastly faces buzzing in my skull, I no longer hated Simon, I knew he really cared about me and I realized the harm he didn't mean to cause, he was to young to even notice it was me all along, I messed up everything I destroyed the things that couldn't be destroyed, I ruined the things which were already ruined, and I felt sick for it sick in my soul and in my mind, all I ever wanted was to be loved to have a family that cared that treated me like I was a pot of gold or some valuable treasure but I was none of that and I knew that I would never get those things.

Chapter 13

master comes to me

By now I had been in the institute for five years, slowly rotting away decaying like spoiled food, never talking and never caring, the doctors pulled me into their offices to talk about my sudden change of mood, but never did I once actually hear what they were saying, all the world around me was quite, blank and filled with a never lasting darkness filling every corner and enclosing me, suffocating me in every way possible. Father stopped by a few times to ask how I was doing, and if I wanted anything special but I still didn't utter a word I just didn't care anymore I knew I hurt him so badly and I wanted to take it all back but it was to late, I was on a road to destruction and I didn't even care. I asked to stay in my room during each day but was denied, the doctors threatened that if I stayed in my room I would only harm myself, they claimed that I needed to interact with the other kids, and that if I stayed silent any longer I would be moved to the pads, I still didn't care though seriously what real harm was I actually doing to myself? As threatened I was moved to the pads, I sat in the corner and didn't move by the end of the week I had a pile of trays with untouched food, luckily I wasn't put into the jacket, only stuck in that room to suffer and think about what I was doing, which was absolutely nothing. Frankly I didn't understand what good putting me in this room was doing I was now even more alone and in a way I got my wish, and I laughed at the thought of it. I was I the pads for about three weeks, soiling myself once again when I had no will left to hold it in, and when I was finally let out I stunk and was immediately given a bath. The doctors came to an anonymous conclusion that even they couldn't make me talk, and locking me up wasn't doing crap, so they just ignored me and my behavior, which was fine with me because no matter what they did I still wouldn't talk, over time, I lost the will to even try to talk with anyone, so I was now voiceless and it didn't bother me the least bit. I sat in the same chair during recreational time everyday, by myself throughout the day, wasting away like some old person, time slowly dragging me under, so much that I could no longer breathe. After a while the doctors stopped caring all together, they claimed I was a waste of time and that they were disgusted with me and all that I represented, but still I didn't care they too were a waste of time to me, all that they promised me and all that they claimed that would make me better was nothing but shit, not a thing just false hope. Still Simon wrote me letters and after a while I forgot how to put the letters together to form even the simplest words, I skimmed through the letters and they just didn't make any sense to me, so I asked the nurse to recite it to me, he had only read a few words until he babbled on about, his average day and that he was going to school and that he had accumulated more friends and that he really loved his new family, he told me of his stupid mistakes and his new pets, he informed that mother had stopped by a couple of times and that he still loved her no matter what she had done, and once she was done reciting the note, I broke down in tears, once again he had everything I didn't have and the hate I once had for him, jumped back into my mind and soul once again igniting a plan to rid of him, for once and for all. As long days passed, and the months took their place years came into play. The institute discovered a new treatment called shock therapy, it wasn't anything to be proud of the doctors applied several wires tapped to your temples they then it would shoot electricity through out your head hoping that it would cure what problems you had, glad I hadn't had it yet, but I knew it was coming up soon. The next few weeks went by very slow, like usual I moped around the institute never once saying a word; I can't describe how much I wanted death and just a single moment of peace from this place. I was so small to the world, and it bugged me knowing all my life's work had been destroyed by a simple act of realism; I just couldn't grasp the point of knowing that no one believed me, and how they consistently called me Adam, I wasn't Adam no matter how messed up I was, I knew who I was and I wasn't him, I would never allow myself to stoop down to his level. The day went by fairly quickly and before I knew it I was in my room staring up at the ceiling with a blank mind. Once again I sat in the recreational room alone speechless and blank minded, a small boy came over to me and asked if I wanted to play chess with him, but I didn't reply I ignored him and closed my eyes, he shrugged his shoulders and walked away as if he really wanted me to play with him, but I knew that one of the doctors must have put him up to it, and I laughed at the sight of it seriously no matter how hard they tried I refused and by the end of the day I must have been asked at least ten times to play by random kids. But I refused every time and disregarded everyone that asked. Its raining out and all though I cant see it I can hear it, I listen as it hits the tin roof and splashes off giving a drumming noise to the inside of the asylum, my mind is buzzing and in a way I felt sick, a little bit sicker than usual my head was sweaty and my knees began to shake and I constantly heard someone calling my name, I look around and find nothing, just the grey concrete and peeling of the white painted walls, the asylum had a strong musky smell and sadly it makes me ill, as I sit in my usual spot in the recreational room alone and silent, but once again I hear it calling me by my name, who or what I haven't got a clue, but its driving me nuts, it constantly rings in my ears and it replays like a broken record in the back of my head, I shake my head hoping trying to make it stop but it only increases louder and louder until it's at a full yell I lash out and scream what, but it doesn't answer only repeats itself over and over again. I can hear the ticks and tocks of the clock in the hall and the sound can drive you mad at times, but I'm use to it so it doesn't bother me that much, I watch it as time slowly goes by and it would seem that today has been going by rather slowly slower than usual, the rain left the air in the institute damp to were it merely chills my bones, and makes me shiver. I'm freezing and I can hardly feel my toes, as if they aren't even their anymore and I'm quite tired and my eyes are like lead they constantly shut but open at times, but I cant sleep no matter how hard I try, and when I'm almost asleep they flash open, causing me to jump in bewilderment and annoyance my mind is throbbing and I no longer can stay still, once again I hear my name being called repeatedly and its frustrating so I scan the areas around me and still I see nothing, I'm nervous at the moment and its making me sick to my stomach, I just want it to stop I want what ever or whom ever is calling my name to come out and tell me what they want and why they call me constantly. I'm sure that will never happen though no matter how many times I call the one whom speaks my name I never get an answer back only silence and mere mumbles, while I lye in my bed that night I met a person, he or she came into my room, but I couldn't see his or her face, the darkness blinded me so I was kept in a miserable suspicion of who or what is was, I sat up and called out into the darkness but didn't get a reply, so I walked towards the shadow with out stretched hands and felt my way around the room twice but never did I find that person whom came to me and it made me angry and scared, and by the middle of the night I saw it again, it was walking towards me and it seemed like it had glowing red eyes and ivory white teeth, I quickly bolted under my blankets hoping that the material would save me and keep me save and out of harms reach at least that is until morning, but I seriously doubted it, whatever it was it wanted me and I knew it would stop at nothing to get me, so I stayed under the blankets, and before I knew it, whatever it was, sat upon my bed beside me and whispered my name, I shook in fear and trembled non stop, I wanted it to go away and when I made an attempt to tell him to leave I received a vicious laugh, its hand skimmed my face and stopped at the edge of the blanket covering my face, I tightened my grip and promised myself I wouldn't look, but it was so tempting and in an instant I uncovered myself and beside me sat an angle of a man black wings cascaded from his back and he had snow white hair which fell at his shoulders, he glowed with pure beauty and a

I gasped at the sight, it wasn't a monster as far as I could tell but I knew whatever this man was he wasn't a friend to me but a scoundrel. I only sat in silence hoping him would leave but he didn't move or blink he just stared at me, and frequently chuckled under his breath, when I tried to hide under the blankets again, I received a loud screech which delivered a painful blow to my ears, I quickly backed away and before I knew it I was at the end of the bed and he had come closer almost to where he was in my face, go away I screamed once more terrified while shaking in fear, but the only reply it gave was another laugh, it reached out and grabbed me by the neck and squeezed, I tried to push him away but it was to strong for my weak self, and when I grabbed his hand it burned me and I screamed instantly, but he didn't let go only tightened his grip to where I no longer could breath and the second I blacked out I awoke in the fiery deeps of hell, the air was filled with a deep fog and nothing was visible, screams of terror rung in my ears and I heard cries of please and help, accompanied by evil laughs. The sky was red and fire circled around me, and when I touched it my hands began to bleed and my body doubled over in a horrid pain. I fell to my knees and screamed but only cries of those in agony answered, 'help' I screamed aloud, 'someone help me please' I shouted but never had a spoken reply only more cries and screams. As the fog slowly vanished I saw a miserable sight, people were covered in blood locked up in cages which were slowly being lowered into red hot lava while demons feasted on the decapitated bodies of unfortunate humans, I screamed at the sight of it and closed my eyes in fear, and in that instant a hand grabbed my shoulder and called my name, and when I opened them it was the beast from my room and then I realized it was him the devil, it wasn't human of any kind but a deformed demon and upon its head sat two horns, it smiled the same pointy toothed smile and tightened its grip on my shoulder, I quickly fell in pain but it pulled, me up with great force. My eyes filled with tears and my forehead balled with sweat, "what do you want from me"? I begged. But it only smiled and pushed me foreword and in front of me in a cage was me covered in blood and as I focused I noticed that I had no face and no limbs just my torso with an empty head, I screamed at the sight of it and closed my eyes, but its hand squeezed my face causing me to flinch, I opened my eyes and watched as the boy in the cage was slowly removed by a demon it drug me to a pot and stuck me in it, they were going to eat me and I would have to watch. "No". I screamed and turned away. "Yeesssssss" It laughed then turned my head back towards the awful scene before me. I shook my head in terror I wanted to wake up I wanted to be back in the institute, its hands seized the nape of my neck and shook me viciously to the point of where my body fell completely numb until I no longer was able to move. It then with me in its hands walked to the edge of a cliff, I struggled and cried I pleaded for it to let me go, and to my plead it did it dropped me off the edge and I fell with great speed, and when I hit the bottom I awoke in the institute back in my room all alone, but I still looked around searching for him, but fortunately I didn't find him, and for a minute I thought that I must have dreamt the whole thing, but I looked down at myself and I was saturated in a great amount of blood and my hands were burned and blistered from touching the fire. I instantly froze and a scream escaped my mouth, and seconds later a nurse barged in she flashed me a look of concern, "Adam what happened"? She asked quickly. My legs buckled underneath me and I then collapsed to the ground, she was at my side and the room seemed to blur together colors flashing around me like I was spinning and behind her stood the angle his wings outstretched he smiled and then suddenly vanished. I awoke in the nurses room, a turquoise blanket covering me, I slowly lifted the blanket to find I was dressed in a paper gown, I quickly sat up and searched the room for the nurse but she was no where to be found, so I lied back down and closed my eyes, I had been to hell and back in one night and it left me exhausted and drenched in fear. I awoke again in the same spot but when my vision cleared I noticed he stood before me his black wings at his sides, I bolted up and stared at him, "what is it you want with me"? I demanded angrily. he smiled and took my hand in his and in an instant I was back in hell again, once again it looked the same, a thick fog once again soaked the skies and screams rang in terror, I quickly stood up and looked for him, and before I knew it a hand clinched the back of my neck which instantly made me fall, but like before he pulled me to my feet, the thick fog cleared and in front of me stood me, I was older and nothing seemed to be missing like before but in my hands lye Edith and Edgar both limp and covered in blood and before my feet sat a knife covered in blood, I screamed and turned away to look at him, "I demand to know why you are doing this to me"? I screamed. But as my gaze flittered to him and I found my eyes gawking at him, he wasn't the young angle of a man I had seen back in the institute but a horrendous monster with razor sharp teeth and a body masked in pure red, he was the devil, and for some radical reason he had come to me. And then he talked it was the first time I had ever herd him speak and it came out in a sharp ear piercing scream, "I brought the here to show him what hell is and how the will soon become". He laughed. I fell to the floor and cradled myself rocking back and forth crying like a baby, he quickly lifted me up by my shirt and threw me in front of him, by then the fog cleared and a sea of blood lied before me, and as I looked into it faces stared up at me with black eyes and yawning mouths, I screamed and backed away, but he kicked me foreword again and with one slight shove he delivered I fell in, no mater how hard I tried to swim to the edge I only drifted further and further away, the smell burned my senses and made me puke in my mouth, then something grabbed my leg and before I knew it I was submerged under the blood. I gasped for air and struggled and it wasn't long before I floated in the middle of the blood sea, fighting for air whatever had my leg had let go and left me their to suffer and inhale the blood, the blood seemed to thicken concreting me in to the point of where I no longer could move. I screamed but only bubbles escaped, I knew I was dying and I also knew I wanted it, and in a flash I died. I awoke in the middle of the hallway, and like before I was drenched in blood and in my hand was a knife, it fell from my hand and hit the floor with a loud clash, I slowly turned to look behind me and on the ground covered in blood throat slit was the nurse that helped me, I instantly screamed and ran the other way but collapsed at the feet of a doctor he flashed me a look of concern and kneeled down beside me, "Adam what on earth is going on"? He demanded. I tried to talk but only mumbles came out, so I took his hand and pulled him towards the dead nurse, and once I got to the spot I found nothing, I quickly looked at my clothes which to my complete surprise their wasn't a speck of blood on me. I flashed him a concerned look, "she was right here". I replied in a short breath. He shook his head and sighed, "Who was right here"? He asked sarcastically. "The nurse she was dead, I saw her she was right here". I sputtered. He sighed and shook his head, "Adam I don't know what you are talking about, no one is here". He gasped. "But I saw her doctor; she was right here dead, believe me she was here". I cried. He shrugged his shoulders and smiled, he escorted me back to the nurse's office, and in a chair back turned towards me was the nurse that I had seen dead minutes ago. She turned towards us as the door shut with a click, "Adam where have you been, I've been looking for you"? She demanded in a serious tone. I sighed and sat down, "no where sorry". I replied. The doctor gave her a sad look and left. She walked towards me and sat beside me, "Adam what is going on with you". She asked concerned. I slowly shrugged my shoulders and looked at the ground. She rubbed the back of my neck and smiled, "well whatever it is I'm sure you'll tell me soon so I won't badger you any more". She replied. I nodded and smiled, "might I go to my room"? I asked under my breath. She smiled, "why don't you go to the recreational room"? She asked. I sighed, "I'm tired right now". I muttered. She nodded, "sure, just go lye down, and I'll see you soon". She replied. I nodded and went to my room; I slowly lied down and drifted off into sleep". But a voice interrupted me, "you can call me master". It spoke. I turned and he was beside me, his ivory hands folded in his lap, I jumped in fear, "please don't hurt me". I begged, he laughed an ear piercing snicker, "no Adam I won't hurt you I only want to show you". He chuckled. I gave him a strange look, "what is it you want to show me"? I asked desperately. He smiled and took my hand in his, and once again I was in hell. The fog was gone and all round I could see people being tortured, I gasped at the sight and buried my face in my hands, I no longer wanted to see what was in front of me it was tearing me apart thread by thread, and soon the last would be pulled and I would evaporate at once. He pushed me forward an inch and in front of me stood me again, but this time I carried a baby, its carcass was twisted and mangled dripping wet in velvet blood, I screamed at once and looked away but he immediately turned my face to look, by then the picture had changed, instead of the baby in my hands was rose, her body was limp and pale, he eyes starred up at me and her lips were covered in dried blood, I watched as I dropped her and as she hit the ground she turned to ash. I didn't understand what it all meant, I would never hurt her of the twins ever, they were all I had. He laughed behind me and turned my body around, "do you see now"? He screeched. I nodded, but in reality I didn't, none of it made any sense to me. He smiled and nodded, "look now". He replied. I turned again, and in front of me was Simon, he was young, and was crying I looked at my master, "and what does it mean"? I begged, he sighed "he is your brother is he not"? He asked confused. I nodded but with hesitation, he chuckled, when you see your kids or your wife you cry but when you see him you don't, why is that"? He muttered. I sighed, "I do not love him". I choked out. He smiled and patted my head, *"take revenge on those who love you, not on the ones who have hurt you"*. He replied. I gave him a serious look, "that doesn't make any sense". I replied in confusion. He chuckled, "you soon will Adam, you soon will". He said then he vanished and once again I was back in my room. *"Take revenge on those who love you, not on the ones who have hurt you"?* I didn't understand what that meant, why would I hurt the ones I loved instead of the ones who hurt me? It didn't make any sense, but I would do as he said no matter if it didn't make sense he was my master and I would follow him. Through out the night my mind had been poisoned rage circled through my veins and hate ignited for rose and the twins, I hated them so much and once I was free I would kill them all, I finally grasped what he had showed me, and when I thought about it, I found that it was clearer than glass, the things I saw was what was going to happen it was my future and I was going to fulfill it to the end of time". But I also had to take into consideration that I was still a young kid of twelve and I would have to be fortunate to even find them, but when I did I would end them all, and fast. And the thought of it made me a little sick, but it's what my master wanted and instructed me to do, so I would follow through. Master visited me hourly everyday he was like my shadow, in my very steps his breath tickling the back of my neck every second his voice replaying in the back of my head. After the last showing of hell, he never once took me back, and I never again saw his monstrous form again, which didn't bother me the least bit, I preferred seeing him in his sinister angle like form, it gave me comfort and relieved my constant stress, and to be honest he was the prettiest man I had even set eyes on. Master promised me that if I did what he said he would grant me eternal life and happiness for the end of times, he said that he would make me the luckiest man alive and that no one would be able to resist me. Occasionally he whispered things into my ear like how brilliant I was and how I was his perfect candidate for what he had planned, and when I asked what he had planned he only chuckled, I wanted to know this plan he had for me but I knew he wouldn't tell me until I finished my first few tasks. Every night when I went to bed I dreamt of him, and what he had promised me and how happy I would be when I got it. he instructed me to eat more and that I would need my strength for what was about to happen, but I didn't know what was even going to happen, but I did as he said I ate and ate until my stomach was about to explode, and he made it able for me to sleep again. Master was a sinister man no doubt, but he saved me and gave me another life, a life of promise and opportunity to redeem myself and it gave me hope and joy to know that I had been given a chance to fix the wrong I had done. I slept every night and ate every meal, even if the food made me gag or gave of a retched stench I still consumed every bite, but with a great deal of hesitation. Master hasn't come to me today and I'm worried that I did something wrong, so I'm redoing every thing to make absolute sure I don't let him down, because I love him and he is all I have. I didn't sleep tonight I only lied in bed and waited for him to show up to praise me for the rights I have achieved, but he never did. And it made me worry until my head throbbed and I felt extremely sick, I fell to the floor in shame, I couldn't understand why he hadn't come to me, had he forgot about me, did I do a wrong of some sort? I didn't know and I badly wanted to. For a split second I closed my eyes and lied back on my bed and dreamt myself bowing before my master and he slowly lifted me up and put a glass of blood into my hands and told me to drink, and that if I did it would give me eternal life and riches beyond belief, and so I drank and drank but every time my cup emptied it began to fill itself up again, so I continued to drink but the cup never emptied only filled itself up over and over again.

Chapter 14

good vs. evil

A bright light exploded through my door and into my room tonight and I immediately thought it was master so I called his name, but was only laughed at, but I knew it wasn't masters laugh but a sweet kind laugh, I dashed out of bed and walked towards the light, and as I got closer I saw an angel, she was tall and had black hair with ocean blue eyes, her wings were white and cascaded down to her feet, and above her head a bright white light escaped. I gasped at the sight, she came closer and the light died down. "Are the Adam"? She asked slowly. I nodded, "yes I am". "I am Serpentine, angel of time and good". She replied in a sweet voice. I backed away, "why have you come to me"? I demanded. She smiled, "you are caught up I two worlds Adam, good and evil, I am here to give you the option to make the right decision, and turn towards the light not the dark". She informed. I nodded, "master would not like this right now". I mumbled. She flashed me a look of concern, "this master who is he"? She asked quickly. I fiddled my fingers, "he doesn't want me to say". I replied holding my breath, trying not to show my weakness. She smiled, "this master of yours is he from around here"? She asked. I blinked at the question; he was from hell so yes he was from around here, so I nodded. "Yes . . . from around here". She nodded and sat beside me, "Adam, do not fear me, I do not wish that, I only want you to do the righteous thing". She replied softly. I took what she said and thought about it, "What is your offer"? I asked quickly. She flashed me a concerned look, "what did your master offer"? She asked slowly. I sighed, "Master promised me that if I did what he said he would grant me eternal life and happiness for the end of times, he said that he would make me the luckiest man alive and that no one would be able to resist me". I replied smugly. She smiled and shook her head in pity, "I cannot promise you all that but I can promise you that you will be free of his hold and will no longer have suffer is his presence". She replied. I looked at her quickly, "I do not suffer in his presence and I am free, so you can go now". I retaliated. She smiled, "why do you like him so"? She asked in confusion. I shrugged my shoulders, "because I love him and he looks after me". I said slowly. She sighed, "Before I go I want to show you what it is he is doing and what good it is he's not". She smiled and took my hand in hers and in an instant we were in the recreational room, on the couch sat a girl she was crying and alone, but seconds later two male watchmen came into the room one sat on one side and the other on the other side, to where she was in the middle. I didn't understand what it was he was trying to show me, but I soon found out. One of the guys was short and plump, the other tall and lean both had dark brown hair cut short and tidy. I watched as the fat one slowly put his arm around the weeping girl he whispered something into her ear she then quickly shook her head, he smiled and placed his hand on her breast she quickly shoved it away and tried to stand up but he snatched her back down and grabbed her face in his chubby hand, the other guy had his hand in his pants rubbing his penis he flashed her a smile, he then grabbed her hand and stuck it down his pants and moved it back and forth, the girl was crying and trying to leave but the fat one held her tight so she wasn't able. I watched in disgust as the skinny man got off, he released her hand and slowly put his hand down her pants and also started to move his hand back and forth, her face tightened and she made a low moan, while he was doing this the fat man pulled her face to his and was kissing her forcefully. I so badly wanted to confront the men and help that poor girl, but when I tried I ended up back in my room. I looked at her in anger, "why didn't you stop that you could have stopped it but you didn't" I screamed. She sighed, "its out of my hands Adam, I cannot do anything to help that deprived girl, nor can you. Sure you can go tell the doctors and confront the men and talk to the girl but it wont do any good, *'you can't change the past but you can always alter the future Adam'*. She quoted. I looked at her in rage, "my master would have stopped it". I screamed. She shook her head, "your master did this Adam, he is dreadful he was watching while it happened and he allowed it". She said slowly. I shook my head, "you liar my master would have stopped it, you watched you tolerated it not him". I screamed in resentment. She flashed me a sour look and sighed, "It would seem that you don't want me here, so I'll go but I will be back Adam, indeed I will". At that she vanished and my room became dark quiet and lonely again. I was lost, I can honestly say that now, I loved my master and I also knew he was the devil, and this angel that appeared wanted me to come her way, she was so beautiful and a true angel, but it was so hard yes I wanted to be free of sadness and dept but I owed it to him, I owed him my life and everything I had. I awoke in a panic, I had an awful dream that I saw my master and he took my soul and I was never to be free of him and his wrath, I awoke in tears and drenched in fear and sweat.

She was sitting on the same couch when I saw her as I trotted into the recreational room, I slowly walked towards her she didn't seem to notice her face was red and masked in dried tears, I slowly reached out and touched her hand but she pulled it back and screamed, I flinched away and backed up, she looked at me with wide eyes, "I saw you last night, you were watching me, you saw what happened". She replied angrily. I quickly shook my head, "NO I don't know what you're talking about". I mumbled. She smiled, "I saw you and you didn't help, why you didn't help? I saw you I saw you". I looked at her in confusion; I turned around and behind me stood the angle. "She can see you, how can she see you". I screamed and looked at the girl, by then she was gone. Her hands grasped my shoulders and we vanished. I appeared in a dark room, then like before it exploded in white light. "How did that girl see you"? I asked quickly. She let out a sigh and walked in front of me, "I am an angel Adam, all can see me, you can see me right now what's stopping others from seeing me also"?She asked in a whisper. Her face lit up and she pursed her lips. I looked at her in shock I didn't expect for all to see her just me. "Why are you whispering"? I asked. She smiled, "why are you not"? She replied. I sighed, "Are you going to talk in riddles all the time"? I asked insipidly. She flashed me a quirky smile, "I'm not talking in riddles Adam, and you're just simple that's all". She teased.

"What's the purpose of being here"? I quickly murmured. She let out a frustrated sigh, "look ahead of you". She instructed. As she said I did, in front of me stood a tall scrawny man, his hair hung at matted clumps and as he turned, I nearly choked, I looked at the angel. "Do you recognize this man"? She asked instantaneous. I nodded, "he was my father". I cried. She nodded, "do you see what it is he is doing"? She asked suddenly. I shook my head, "no I don't what is he doing"? She smiled but quickly frowned. "He's giving his soul to the devil and he doesn't even know". She replied. I flashed a confused look. I sighed. "I don't understand". I replied hastily. *'The prince of darkness is always a gentleman, but he who tangles with the devil shall always pay his dues in the end.* She replied with a nod to the head. I nodded and acted like I understood but I didn't, how could I? This angel was talking in riddles and nonsense. She smiled and once again vanished. I opened my eyes to being back in my room, I sat on my bed and buried my face between my blankets, I wanted this to stop, all the games which were being played with me, I hated it, I resented everything and one, and my master even more. I must be in a dream because the walls around me are crumbling at my feet and the ground is tilted and the world is spinning like I'm going to fall off all together. All around the world is covered in a thick blanket of snow, the plants decayed and brown from the freezing cold. I am naked, my feet are buried under the snow and I am shaking, and when I move the world shifts knocking me into the white powdered snow. It chills me and when I look at my hands I notice that they are black frozen and completely dead. I scream out in panic but the answer of howling wolves reply, the world around me is like an ocean of snow and I am stuck dead in the middle I'm struggling to move but I cannot I'm frozen to the ground thick ice inclosing my ankles, concreting me to the earth. My legs and feet have now become a thick chunk of ice and when I break a piece off, it reforms but harder thicker and colder. I can feel my hair stiffen as the harsh breeze chills my back and rattles my bones, I want so badly to give up, the cold is making me tired and the snow is falling in large chunks, so I purposely fall back the snow catching my fall like a cushion, I shiver and my teeth chatter, I'm giving up now I can no longer go on so I just lye still and wait for the wolves to find me and devour me whole or the snow to swallow me up in one gulp. As I lye their the cold creeps in deeper to where I no longer can keep my eyes open, my lungs had frozen not allowing me to breath and I swallow my tongue at once. I am dying I know this now, and when I realize tears pour from my eyes, I do not wish to die, not now at least. Before me the angel appears *'surrender to god. But resist the devil, and in the blink of an eye he shall impart your soul and all'*. She whispered then vanished. I awake in my room on the ground and I instantly dart to my bed, I tunnel under the blankets and close my eyes and drift off into a deep sleep. The sun is high and I can feel sand in between my toes, I'm in a desert the world is quiet and I'm alone, once again I am naked and the sun is constantly beating down on me burning my back and blistering my legs. There are no trees here only small shrubs and cactuses I'm dehydrated and I'm seeing mirages, like pools of water and tables of delicious food. But as I tried to run to it, it would vanish before my eyes, I was dying of heat, and it seemed like the temperature was only increasing until the sun was following me every step shining its deadly rays upon me causing me to go up in flames. I dug a hole in the sand and as I tried to hide in it, it instantly caved in, so I sat down and waited for my guardian angel to save me from this horrid nightmare. If the angel did not come then my master certainly would, I depended on both of them and if they didn't come soon I would evaporate shortly. It wasn't long before my body was covered in a thick layer of sand and when I brushed it off, it would only pile up higher and faster. So I just lied still and waited for it to swallow me whole. My eyes had become heavy and I no longer was able to keep them open so they closed and I gradually drifted off into a deep slumber. *'The devil aids his servants for a spell, but when he is done with them he casts them aside to burn in his own hell*. A voice called. I opened my eyes to the angel; she was kneeling beside me with a wide eyed expression. *'Tell your master the truth and what you want, only then can you be free of his grasp'*. She chuckled. I looked at her irately. "What do these dreams mean"? I demanded. She shrugged her shoulders, "that's for you to decide, you must comprehend them your own way Adam, it's the only way". She replied on the spur of the moment. I awoke in my room again, clothed and drenched in sweat. I stood up and looked around. "I hear you've made a new friend". A voice called out. "Angel is that you"? I asked quickly. "Well you can call me an angel if you'd like". It replied. "Master is that you"? I called out. Then out of the darkness he appeared. "Yes it's me" . . . **Satan was now at hand'**. I glanced at him slowly, "you've not showed up for several days master, what have you been doing"? I asked. He let out a fierce laugh. "I've been here all along, watching you, watching that dreadful angel, how sad that you had to confide in a soul like hers, sure she is sexy but she is a woman and dare not trust her". He laughed. I looked at him bitterly, "she is no bad soul it's you that is". I screamed. He smiled, 'you dare challenge me how, unwise of you'. He said in rage, his perfect form shifting into his deeper monster. "You have done nothing but lied to me, you have betrayed me and taken every bit of good I once had and turned it into sin". I screamed. He stood up and walked towards me, *'you think you are wise speaking to me in such tongue but I'll have you know your soul is mine Adam'.* He chuckled viscously. *I looked at him in rage, "I owe you nothing be free of me you monster, I have* turned to god now". I screamed. He only laughed though, "what god? There is no god, not here not ever, you have only me Adam, your soul is mine and so are you". He replied. "I never gave you my soul, so it is not yours to take". I replied hastily. He smiled, "no Adam I think you're surly mistaken, your soul is mine, and yes you did give it to me". He laughed. I looked at him in concern, "you lie, I never gave my soul to you and I never would". I screamed. He smiled and shook his head, "oh Adam you have no idea what's going on do you"? He laughed. I stared at the ground and kicked the floor, "obviously not, so why don't you fill me in". I said sarcastically. He sighed and smiled, "how about you just find out on your own Adam". I gasped and stared at him "no how about you just tell me, I'm tired of these games you're playing with me, and I'm fed up with the things you're doing". I screamed. He came closer and his perfect form shifted into the monster I so badly wanted to never see again, "now you listen to me Adam, you will tell this angel to go away, you are mine and only mine, do you understand? I am in charge now, you will do as I say or I will make every waking hour a living hell for you". He screamed. I quickly nodded, "yes sir". I replied. He stood up tall and grabbed me by the neck, "you call me master do you get that, I am your master, so you will address me by master". At that he threw me down and vanished. I sat on the cold ground for what it seemed was eternity, I was so scared, he said he had my soul he claimed I was his, and his only but I so badly wanted free from him and all that he claimed he promised. It wasn't long before my angel appeared in the nick of time, "Adam he came to you didn't he"? She replied knowing the answer before hand. I nodded, "he told me to tell you to go away and that I was his and only his". I cried. "Do you want me gone Adam? If so just say the words and I'll go". She mumbled. I quickly grabbed her arm, "don't leave me, please don't leave me, I can't handle this anymore, I'm begging you don't go, your all I have now". I begged. She quickly flashed me a look of concern, "I won't go Adam unless you wish it, but you have to fight him, you can't give in, if you do he will take everything from you". She replied in a low voice. "What's to take? He already has everything". I screamed. She smiled, "not everything Adam". She muttered. I looked at her warily, "what do you mean"? I asked quickly she smiled, "you still have your soul Adam, and you still have that". She replied instantly. "No he claims I gave it to him". I cried again. She shook her head, "Adam your soul is what brought me to you, the one thing that shined from you, so strong and so bright, and I can see that you still have it now". She said in a high voice. I looked at her in shock, "you saw my soul?" I stuttered she nodded, "yes Adam I saw your soul, and I most defiantly can tell its still with you". "Adam your soul is the only thing keeping you here". She replied. I glanced up at her and sighed, "What should I do know"? I asked in melancholy she sighed and patted my back, "don't give him your soul but play him as he has played you". She responded in laughter. I looked at her in shock, "how so? I mean how should I play him"? I asked in a serious tone. She sighed and shrugged her shoulders, "that once again is up to you and you alone, this is your problem Adam not mine". She replied hastily. "I understand it is my problem but I most definitely don't want to tango with the devil". She smiled and squeezed my shoulder, "Adam do you believe in god"? She asked instantly. I looked up at her and sighed, "I'm no sure if I do" I replied staring at the ground. "If you don't believe in god Adam you cannot be saved". She replied hastily. "Satan is a fallen angel Adam, once great and prosperous but turned bad and was casted out of heaven, he does not care for you or are anyone, he's a collector of souls and he wants yours badly, Adam he feeds on your energy, the more you fear, him the stronger he grows, and right now you're feeding him". He whispered gradually. "So what should I do"? I asked quickly. She sighed and scratched her head, "do the righteous thing Adam and you will be free of him and his presence". She chuckled vaguely. "What is the righteous thing to do right now"? I asked in spitefulness, irritation gradually creeping up my spine. He smiled and walked towards the door, "I'll leave that up to you to decide, I'm sure you'll make the right decision". She bellowed. I looked at her and stepped foreword, "and what if I don't make the right choice, than what will happen"? I asked on the threshold of tears. She smiled and opened her wings, "I have no doubt in you Adam, chase your heart and you will do no further harm to yourself or anyone". She whispered than vanished. I slowly shuffled to my bed and lied back; I closed my eyes and drifted off into a ghastly nightmare. It began with me on a small island in the middle of know where, surrounded by a vast ocean of clear glass water.

But then all went dark and clouds enclosed me and the island, heavy rain fell and lightening struck the trees, and they collapsed instantly causing flying embers to burn me. I quickly jumped into the water but by then it wasn't water instead it had become a large pit of sand and snakes were slithering out of it, I quickly backed up but as I did they came closer and faster. The skies had become red and the moon shined in small beams, I wasn't in hell or in heaven but in the in-between and I finally grasped the concept of these dreams and the real meanings of them, it was me all along, I was stuck not in the fiery depts. Of hell or the divine love of heaven but caught in the in-between, between good and evil and I knew I had hardly any time left to make the decision of where to be and which to turn to and if the decision didn't come soon I would forever be caught in the middle. I awoke in panic, sweat balled on my forehead and my limbs shook, I slowly sat up and looked around, the room was still casted over by the darkness, and fear grew in the pit of my stomach igniting a longing for death and escape. Hope no longer fueled my madness but instead anger, the deepest and the most ruthless resentment, it masked my face and my movements, and I had become a vicious careless animal, without a way to tame. I no longer heard the constant calling of my name, it brought joy to the sliver of heart I still had, but not enough to power the hope and assurance I so badly yearned for. I was a spineless pathetic excuse for a human, and I knew it and no mater how hard I tried to be good again; I would instantly disintegrate like ash. No one cared for and about me, I was invisible and completely mute to all eyes and all ears, I missed my family, I longed to see Aurora's beautiful face or to gaze upon the twins and even more my Elizabeth. At times I swear I could see her face in my dreams as if she was my guide, I missed them badly and I knew that even hope would never grant me that. I was a lost soul I the already lost world, go figure. I have one more month before my release date, and once the news rung in my skull I sulked to my knees and cried like a baby, I was finally getting out, atlas I would be free. Every day seemed as if it went by at two miles per hours, but I waited still and lingered in the recreational room alone like usual. Master came to me during the night, he sat upon my bed and laughed in my face, I looked up at him in rage, "what are you laughing about"? I demanded. He smiled, "do you actually think your getting out of here"? He chucked. "What do you mean? I asked in fear. "You're never getting out Adam, not now not ever, your trapped this is your home". "You're wrong, I am getting out, and the doctors said I was to be released in a month". I cried in assurance. He sighed, "Take my word for it you are never getting out of this place". He laughed. "Why don't you just go away, I have no need for you, and frankly you're not wanted"? I screamed. His eyes grew red, and he bared his sharp teeth and he stood up, "think what you want, but I know the truth, so if I were you I'd just forget about freedom and consider this your home". He demanded. "But I will go, because you claim you don't want me here, but their will be a time when you do and I will be at hand". He laughed then vanished into the musty air. I cried that night, I cried until no tears came out, I curled myself into a ball and rocked back and forth, what if what he had said was true, that I wasn't getting out of here, what if I was never to be free? The thought burned my head and made me double over me fear and nausea. I had to get out, they couldn't keep me here forever and that was that. 'He's lying, he's just trying to scare me, he is the devil that's what he does he lies' I muttered, in assurance. 'The devil himself is the author of lies and confusion'. Or that's what the angel had said. The second I was let out of my room I asked to see the psychiatrist, she took me into her room with confusion, "what is it Adam"? She asked coldly. "I was wondering when my let out date was"? I asked slowly. She smiled and let out a deep sigh, "Adam, who said you were to be let out"? She quickly asked. My eyes grew wide, "the doctors said I was to be out in a month". I cried. She shook her head, "I have nothing about that in my papers, and maybe you're mistaken". Anger swelled in my gut and I needed a way to lash out, either I'd bite her head off or I would turn her inside out. "You're lying I'm getting out, why are you doing this?" I screamed. She gave me a crucial look, "watch what you say Adam, you're not getting out, this is your home now so you'd better get use too it, and just forget about leaving, now go to your room". She demanded. "I'm getting out of here, you just watch, I will I promise you that". I yelled then left. I slowly trotted into my room and flopped down on the bed, "was I right or was I right, I told you that you weren't getting out". Master chuckled from the corner of the room. I buried my head under my pillows, "just go away and leave me alone". I cried through muffled screams. He smiled and clicked his tongue, "fine I'll go if that's your wish, but like I said I will be back". He laughed then instantly vanished. I closed my eyes and drifted off into a deep slumber. The next day went like it came, slow and motionless, I reassured myself that I was getting out and that the psychiatrist was just off her rocker and forgot about it, I slowly paced around the recreational room back and forth back and forth until I heard a voice. "Don't give up Simon, don't you even consider it, you've been through to much to give up now". It said I a hushed whisper, I quickly looked around only to find nothing, the room had become vacant just me standing in the middle once again alone, the bell must have rung, but then again I never heard it. "Who is that?" I lashed out instantly. "No one, just me, don't you give up". It replied again. I quickly turned around, but no one was their, I was the only one in that room, "what do you want? I demand that you show yourself". I screamed. But a childish chuckle was all I received. "This isn't funny, so come out and show yourself". I cried in unease. Shadows danced across the walls, and laughter filled every corner. I collapsed to my knees and balled myself up; I rocked back and forth, and buried my face in my knees. "Don't cry Simon, why are you crying? Are you a baby?" it asked in sarcasm, I jumped to my feet and ran towards the voice, "go away, and leave me alone". I screamed. "Now why would I do that? I want to be your friend Simon, just a friend". It laughed. Then all at once I was hit over the head, I awoke to bright lights and loud music, I jumped up. The room was dark, cold quite and gave off an eerie chill. I picked myself up off the solid floor and focused in on my surroundings, cold air was being pushed in through a small hair line crack on the closest wall closest to me, I slowly ran my hand over it cold air chilled it so I slowly stuck my eye on it but I couldn't se anything only dark, and all hope had emptied from my bones and brain. I then carefully placed my hands upon the cold cement walls and felt my way around the room, I slowly grasped a metal door knob and tried to open what I had imagined was a door but it didn't budge, I licked and screamed at it until the room flooded in with radiant white light blinding me for a split minute and causing me to fall upon the floor. "Do not panic dear child all is good you are safe, I only want to help you will you let me help you"? It sang. "Who are you and why do you want to help me"? I screamed in anger. "I am Gabriel, angel of life and death, good and bad and the final determination" he sang loudly. I quickly backed away, "what do you want from me"? I stuttered in terror. White teeth smiled and he inched foreword. "Make a decision and make it now for tomorrows to late you'll be under the ground". He sang with fiery red eyes. "What decision, I don't understand"? I yelled back "life or death, heaven or hell, make the decision or you'll be dead". He screamed in anger. "Please". I begged, "heaven not hell, please I don't want to die I want to live". I screamed in sadness. His eyes penetrated my soul and made me shake uncontrollably, and an evil laugh escaped his locked lips. "You lie to me boy you are evil and that of a sinner, I cast you out of heaven, and to hell that is where you will reside forever". He screamed then vanished. I awoke to the walls around me crumbling at my feet, blood pouring down them making them in a red blanket, the room flooded with blood all the way up to the rim of my bed, and in an instant I fell from my bed into the sea of blood before me, I thrashed about trying to keep my head above the red death, my head then went under, the blood traveled up my nose and into my mouth, and trickled down my throat, I choked instantly and spat it out but it only filled my mouth more. My eyes blinked rapidly and by then my room up to the ceiling was filled with the blood, and I was drowning in it, my head completely submerged, blood now concreting my lungs, sealing my lips and finally taking my breath. I reached out and once more thrashed about, I kicked my legs and swung my arms but then I froze and no longer was able to move. I was frozen in the abyss of blood and there was noting I could do about it. Wishing, for life, but hoping for death. I no longer cared, I was going to hell anyway, so it didn't matter if I died now or later, either way I was going to the same place. I no longer had any morals left in my damaged soul, call it self pity or a yearning for sympathy, call it what you will, but honestly I wanted neither of those things just death and all that it invited. I dreamt I died today; I awoke in along narrow box, enclosed on all sides, I listened as earth was being shoveled upon it, I was dead yes, but on the inside I was alive more than I had ever been. My nails scratched at the top of the wooden box, they split and broke causing a pool of blood to form on my chest, above me the shoveling had stopped and a prayer was being muttered, then the lid opens and I am still inside but upon a grand stage, flowers of all colors enclosing my coffin, and small rings and bracelets have been carelessly thrown in, yet my body it still frozen, but I can see all hear and smell all, I scream out in terror, but even as they come up to me and place more flowers around they ignore me and my screams. Above me is a statue of an angel her hands in prayer form, but her eyes flicker open and her hands go up and cover her mouth, but her eyes grown wider and wider and stare straight through me, as if they are about to fall of her face, I scream at the sight and my body and mind numb all at once. Voices are calling me by my name, people I have never seen before are crying and moaning in loss and sadness, I am dead but in reality I am alive, for I have breath and my heart beats like that of a drum, I am dead pale sunken faced, eyes which have caved in, my cheeks ivory bone and my skin falling away I am a skeleton a white skeleton in an museum for all to see, for I am dead and I envy it so. I am coughing, sneezing, choking crying and laughing, my mind is a vacant wasteland, my insides have shriveled and turned to dust, my existence is being blown away by the cold harsh wind and I allow it, I summon, invite and even call all of hell to take me, take me down to the fiery pits and make me a slave turn me against my will and take the life out of me, for it is my home, heaven I say is a wasted space and lacks reason for existence, for in hell you can reign in power, lust pride and the upmost vanity. And that well, that my friend is what I want, forever and ever until my bones cave in and my skin melts off and I turn to fine ash, hell is my release and I will go their soon. "So you've finally made up your mind"? The angels' voice called from the utter darkness. I adjusted to the dark and sighed, "I have not an option, Raphael claims I will never make it to heaven and that hell is where I must remain for all of times". I cried. "Do you know who Gabriel is Adam"? She asked in a confused tone. I quickly shook my head, "angel of good and bad, and heaven and hell and the final determination". I repeated. She smiled and shook her head, "no Adam, Gabriel is the devil, an angel gone bad kicked out of heaven gods own brother, he has no determination only lies and confusion, he is the angel of death". She replied. I swallowed my tongue and fell upon my knees, "he lied to me, and so does this mean I'm not going to hell and that there is still a chance I can go to heaven"? I asked in doubt. She sighed, "Yes there is a chance but you need to make a decision fast, because the gates of heaven are not always going to be open, like that of hell they are always open, greeting every sinner in joy and pride". She mused, "how is it that I can go to heaven, I must die first". I asked confused. A slight chuckle escaped her ruby lips, "yes you must be dead but before you die, you must admit to your sins, but you must do it in church and for someone to hear, Adam if it is heaven you want then you must work for it, and if you want hell then keep doing what it is you are doing and you will surly end up their". I nodded, "yes I understand, but what if I admit to what I have done and I still don't make it"? I asked in horror. She smiled and shook her head, "it doesn't work that way, if you have done wrong in your life, that makes you a sinner and it is said that you automatically go to hell, that is true but if the devil comes to you and starts to take you away, you admit to your guilt and you will be forgiven". She replied hastily. "But how on earth will I be able to get to a church when I'm in here the whole time"? She smiled, "you'll be out of here soon, I promise you". She muttered. I looked at her in shock, "how do you know that"? I asked in utter confusion. She smiled, "I just do, and that's all you need to know". She said with a smug smile. As the angel left me that night I was burning to the core with excitement. I was to be freed and sooner than I had originally imagined, and the overjoyed feeling of what I would do with my new found freedom plagued my mind in hysteria. The world was at my feet and I felt seven feet tall, towering over all even the tallest sky scrapers, my life was ahead of me and I so badly wanted to just break free right now spread my wings and fly away from this damned place. I wanted freedom but most of all I thrived for blood, not mine of course but the blood of others, the pure raw salty velvet blood of my doomed victims I imagined it in my head and it make me shake with thrill, I wanted it, no I needed it, I had to know that their last breath was taken by my hands, it trilled me filled me with an overpowering sensation of power and want. Death no longer hunted me nor heaven I no longer cared, but the thoughts of killing and what I would give to kill right now, it was all I thought about enclosing my mind in a vast ocean of long lasting darkness and pride; it made me laugh one minute but double over in tears. I wanted it so badly but the thought of being alone in the new world made me shiver with fright and sadness, I was cold and tired and the world made me nauseated and sick to my stomach, by now I'd been locked up in the institute for now over thirty years, my life slipping away every second I closed my eyes so far my life had been nothing but ruins, hate and non stop medications, without the slightest tolerance from anyone. I was hated, despised never loved noticed or even in eth realm of welcomed, I was a fat nasty rat displayed for all to see, out in the open for all eyes to gaze upon, malicious words spat at accompanied by screams of anger and distaste. My very sight onto others was nerve racking and it would seem that my very presence was horrifying and made my viewers vomit uncontrollably in their mouths and to be frank it made me sad and I couldn't grasp the concept of their hatred towards me, I wasn't a nasty person or a cunning creature of any kind so I imagined it was my insides that made them loathe me so.

Seven years later . . . .

Chapter 15

the death of me

I am thirty seven today I have been moved to several institutes but now I finally dwell in a hospital, my entire life has been caged I do not know the outside world and my earliest memory is no more, I am dying and it scares me, Lately I have had these pudding head aches and at times my entire body freezes as if for a split second I am ice and I've concluded that I'm never to be free of this place I am a prisoner now, bounded by the concepts of not being able-bodied, a sick person a demented insane creature. It wasn't long before the doctors reported the bad news that is after several check ups and cat scans and continuous x-rays. "Adam we need to talk they said", I just nodded and listened but in a way I was scared. "Adam after going over your at scans we are sad to inform you that you have aggressive brain tumor, looking back at your earlier cat scans is would seem that this tumor has been slowly eating away at you for now over twenty years and its truly sad that it took this long to treat it I am very sorry". I looked up at them in surprise, "I'm going to die aren't I"? I asked through clenched teeth. The doctors eyes watered for a second and he smiled a bit, "possibly, we don't know how long you have but whatever time you do have make the best out of it" I just nodded and left the room in a slow walk, the second I left the room the tears rushed in all was blurry and I collapsed to the ground in grief, I was dying and I finally knew it now, I had no time left, their was no hope for me but either way I didn't care all concern has been flushed out of my body. My head is constantly pounding, throbbing and causing me to strike it repeatedly, it throbs constantly and at times I freeze up, they claim it's growing all the time and that I don't have long. I suppose this is my end, all my wants have drowned in my ever lasting hope for freedom. I was granted to go to the church today and it lifted my spirits a tad, but not enough, *if I should die before I wake*. Unlike the men, women, and children who whispered those words fearfully, I looked to the rafters. They were covered in sawdust and cobwebs; the tapestries cracked and desecrated from the lack of concern. This church, this haven never cast me out, like it should. If God were watching me now, He would have sent the archangel Rafael on my sinister ways and cut me down where I stood. But He didn't. Perhaps the Book was right; He is forgiving and holds His believers to His heart. He forgets that I am not a respectful or even religious person or even any good but a definite sinner, and that I have killed. Mercifully, accidentally, but still I remain a murderer. I have taken life, and the only one who is allowed to take life is God himself. And yet even though I pray, I receive no answer. No revelation and no vision of my future unfolding. For years I thought that perhaps I have been asking for the wrong questions, demanding the wrong things. And now I sit in this pew, asking for forgiveness but really, I should be asking for something quite different. If I should die before I wake. "Please God," I whisper. "Please. I don't want to die', not now and the thought of death and me leaving forever makes me cry harder and harder, for I do not wish to perish not now at least, I beg god to release me from this pain, I ask for an answer or forgiveness, but he doesn't answer, so I squeeze my hands together in prayer and I get on my knees and prey, I prey and prey until all that comes out of me are tears, I bury my head in my knees and don't move, for I am not forgiven and I will die and slowly. The nurse helps me gather myself up off the ground, she too was crying and she wipes her eyes and pulls me close, she helps me onto the van and heads back to the hospital, I have a variety of pills I have to take, they claim that they might help stop or slow down the cancer, but I doubt it I'm dying and I hate it. I have regular scans of my head daily, and there is no sign of decrease in the size or the speed, it's increasing every second eating away at my brain, and it wont be long before I can no longer move about or eat or think right, I'm falling apart at the seems, and even a needle and thread couldn't mend me back together. My legs seized up today as was walking around the halls in the hospital the doctors make me do regular timed walks hoping it will give me strength, I fall to the ground with a thud and blood rushed out of my ears and nose, the lights dimed to nothing and my eyes closed. I awoke in a hospital bed hooked up to several iv's and meters with flashing light and for a second I imagined they were Christmas lights upon a sparkling tree, but the thought faded and I went into a seizure, the meters buzzed and in rushed several doctors and nurses, they ran around me with flying hands and loud talking, "lift em up, get him stabilized" "hurry get em up, get the defibrillator". A shock rushed through me and I saw white lights just a vast valley of white then blackness and for a second I could see flowers, but as I ran towards it I was pulled back, constantly pulled further back, and as I tried to reach it, it would only back further away until it was miles away, so I ran I ran until I couldn't anymore. Then I awoke, the doctors stood around me and the meter ticked at my heart beat, "welcome back Adam, we thought we lost you". A tall doctor cried in panic, I lifted my lips to a smile but they instantly fell down, and my eyes twitched. They fed me through tubes and all the food tasted the same, a bland taste like mixed vegetables. 'life support' that's what its called, I was now on that just slowly wasting away, I wanted death now no more suffering, I never felt the pain I was constantly drugged on morphine and other pain killers, now I was just sitting their waiting, left to die. Waiting for Gabriel to take me down to hell, waiting for his icy grip upon my shoulder, just left waiting. Mother and Simon came by today with a bouquet of roses, she was old and wrinkly her hair cut short and her face all made up I'm not sure what she was wearing but it seemed like a purple flowered dress, Simon was wearing a suite of black his face was strong and charming his eyes were sad and I could hear his heart tick faster as he neared the bed. mother placed the flowers by the window and sat beside me, Simon beside her she took my hand in hers and caressed it softly, she looked at me with loving eyes "Adam I'm so sorry for what I've done to you, this is my fault all of this and I want so badly to take it all back I wish I could have been a better mother, your dying Adam and I cant do anything about it, you're my son even if I haven't been here for you I want you to know I love you, I always have, so please for my sake Simon's and your fathers tell us about your life before this happened before the institute, please tell me, tell me your adventures your loves your everything". She cried, so with my last hour of life I told her of my life story, I told her about rose and the twins I told her about Elizabeth and aurora, I shared the sins I had done, I told her of the helpless lives I took and the shame and pain it brought upon me, I told her of my loss and my happiness and about prison, I told her everything and with my last moments nearing by I told her I loved her and father and most of all Simon, I watched as tears ran down her old face, and she squeezed my hand in hers and in that second, Simon took my hand in his and upon his face was grief and inside my heart I felt a rush of sanity and yearning for things to go back to the way they were when I had the chance to make things right. Simon held my hand in his and told me that he loved me and would always remember me and in those last seconds I cried for the first time in front of my family and as Simon held my hand in his my eyes closed and my heart stopped ticking. I cant say I went to heaven and nor can I say I went to hell I don't know where I went, I do know that I didn't see fields of flowers or pearly gates, but nor did I see darkness. But one of the several things I did learn was to forgive because a life in anger and jealousy only holds you back and vengeance was what I learned of most, to get revenge on someone is not the way to go but instead learn to forgive and forget because I know now what harm I brought to my family to my wife's and kids and even if none of what I experienced was true or real I don't care I'm just glad that in my last seconds I saw my family again, so I might say that this is the end but if you look at it through my eyes it's only the beginning.